Arcane Mysteries

Magic Guardian Academy
Book 1

Rebecca Goodwin

Secrets, Magic, and Betrayal…all in the first semester!

Zoey is a witch, but she's not very good at it.

That is until she's taken a secret school of mages. There, she discovers a whole new world of a different kind of magic, one that she seems to excel in.

She and three fantastically hot boys who are "keeping her safe" are trying to figure out how she escaped their world in the first place and why her parents hid her.

And they'd better hurry because something is trying to kill her.

Cover Design by Ravenborn Book Cover Designs

Page Break Design: Shutterstock

Title and Chapter Heading Font: Free to use for personal and commercial projects, no additional licensing is needed. www.fontmesa.com FontMesa fonts.

Chapter 1

The metal lockers in front of me vibrated as a body slammed against the other side. *Don't get involved, don't.*

"You're sorry, isn't enough, asshole," a male voice hissed.

My magic prickled across my palms like sharp ice, and I squeezed them shut before anyone else saw my power. Really didn't need to have everyone around me freak out. I tucked the sleeves of my pullover down lower, to cover my fists.

Go to class, Zoey, don't even stop. Except, I never listened to myself, so I rounded the corner. Other students hurried around the trio, their sneaks squeaking across the linoleum, avoiding staring too long at the exchange.

The victim hunched down, curling into himself for protection. His slicked black hair laid flat against his head.

"Give us a reason why we shouldn't shove you into the dumpster," Darren said. "You stared at my girl at the game last night. And sat behind her in class this morning. Think she'd be interested in a cock-sucker like you?"

I rolled my eyes. *Pathetic.* Darren's face twisted into a snarl and made him look more like a red-faced gorilla than he normally did. His girlfriend was a sleaze. Everyone knew that but him, apparently.

The freshman whimpered, his tear-filled eyes pleading as he glanced around for someone—anyone to help him. I had my own problems. Like keeping a low profile and whipping out spells wasn't going to help that.

Darren sucker-punched the freshman in the stomach and the kid crumpled. Then he kicked him, the kid skidded across the floor, banging into the wall of lockers. I thought that would be the end of it except Darren gestured to his friend who hauled their victim upright and he punched him again. The sound of fists on flesh echoed in my ears, and I cringed. A quick glance around showed a crowd was forming around the fight, but no one was doing a damn thing to stop it.

Shit. They were going to beat the kid to a pulp. Gathering my magic in my hand, I strolled past the chaos, a bit too close to Darren and pretended to trip, bumping into the gorilla. With the reflexes of a viper, I slammed a spell across his back, the magic tingling over my flesh, then I staggered back.

"Oh, shit, sorry 'bout that."

"Watch it, bitch!" He shoved me away.

I shrugged, stuffing my headphones into my ears and weaved into the crowd. A few feet away, I paused at Darren's yells, a smirk forming on my lips. His letterman jacket steamed. Black spirals curled up from the yellow and white cloth. My smile widened as he jerked it off, beating it on the floor to smother the flames. But he didn't know shit about magic. Most of the normal folks knew nothing about it. The fire wouldn't stop until my spell was complete and his pants were next. Let everyone see him naked and see what it was like to be laughed at.

"What the fuck, man?" Darren's friend let go of the freshman who then ran away, stumbling.

The familiar hum of electricity surged under my skin again, ready. I'd been thirteen when the ability manifested. I clenched my fists to hold onto the magic and keep it from sparking out and doing more damage like activating the sprinkler system or blow out all the fluorescent lights above me.

I turned to leave, when Darren's girly scream made me spin back around. Now the sizzling flames engulfed his tee too… wait, it was meant to go for his pants. Guess I put a bit too much oomph in my spell than I thought. Oh, well, not like he didn't deserve it and more. He yanked his black T-shirt off, his fellow bully backed away from him now like he was contagious.

"Fuck!" Darren screamed, racing for the water fountain on the other side of me.

White curls of smoke wafted from his hair and eyebrows. His meaty hands splashed water on his face and tried to wet his hair too. The scent of burnt hair clogged the air and I choked. It smelled worse than a run over skunk on a hot, humid day. I gagged, holding my hand over my face as I backed away.

Students raced away from him in every direction. Couldn't

say that I blamed them. Ugh, was the smell getting worse? His friend, terrified, shoved others out of his way as he fled.

"Help me!" Darren shouted with clumps of his brown hair in his hands. He glanced around, his eyebrows gone, and patches of his pale scalp emerged from beneath his locks.

Oops, definitely a little too much magic.

"Sucks to be you." I laughed and continued down the hallway toward my class.

Someone grabbed my arm. I jerked to get free, thinking it was Darren's lackies attacking me. A gorgeous guy with spiked silver hair dragged me away. Still didn't give him permission to manhandle me.

"What the hell?" I popped my earplugs out of my ears.

He didn't answer but pushed me into an empty classroom.

Did he suspect what I'd done? Adrenaline pumped through me, making my skin tight and hot. I spun, ready to fight if I had to, and curled my shoulders forward.

He kicked the door shut behind him, his eyes narrowed on me. Panic squeezed my chest. My magic sizzled across my palms.

"Saw what you did to that guy," he accused.

Panic slammed into me, and that was terrible news for my control. Before I could stop it, my hands buzzed, and a spark shot out from them and slammed into the wall, burrowing a hole into it. The plaster crumbled to the floor. White smoke billowed up from the wall.

"Oh, shit!"

"You think!" His arctic blue eyes glared at me. "Witch!"

My mouth turned to dried paste. Nausea rolled through me and I swallowed hard. *Think, Zoey, think. Make something up. Anything.*

"Wha—you're crazy," I said, keeping my voice level. "That's clearly bad wiring. Not that I'm surprised, this building is older than dirt." God, the principal and the teachers were going to freak about this. Better if I was nowhere near here. Especially since a few feet away, Darren had his clothes and hair dissolve off him. I pushed past handsome, but he blocked my path.

"Yeah, right." The corner of his mouth lifted into a lopsided grin.

My shoulders relaxed some. Sounded like he was going to let this go. No big deal. So a huge hole was now in a classroom wall, so what? Humans didn't know about magic. He had to believe my story, but no need to give him any more info. Didn't want the principal calling me into question about the freaking hole or Darren or the spark that had flown out of my hand.

His grin made me feel lightheaded. The scent of pine and an addictive musk coming from him enveloped me and my feet slipped forward like he called to me. To taste those full lips and see if they were as good as he smelled.

Wait! I shook my head. *What is wrong with me?*

"See you soon, Zoey Dane."

"Wha—" Shock zapped through me. *How did he know my name?*

With a pop, he disappeared into thin air. I stumbled forward, waving my hand back and forth where he'd been standing only seconds ago.

He's a warlock!

Oh, donkey crap. Was he from the Supernatural Council, and I'd just be caught doing magic on humans?

A cold dread filled me because I'd fucked up royally this time.

Chapter 2

Clouds darkened the sun and an icy shiver trailed down my back as I raced home. I couldn't even concentrate on the rest of my classes. My mind still replaying that warlock vanishing before my eyes. I skipped the rest of school, not wanting to deal with anything other than talking to my mom about all the shit that had gone on today. Oak, Pine, and Elm trees along the street shifted with dark limbs as if watching me. Shadows stretched toward me across the concrete. I shuddered, hunching down into my jacket and turning the volume up on my earbuds to block out the sound of my pounding heart.

At my house, I rushed inside, and locked the door behind me. Even though the light leading upstairs was on, the house felt dark. Like the walls pressed in on me. A sensation like a thunderstorm hovered in the air, almost crackling. And it was silent like a cemetery at night. I tugged out my earbuds.

"Mom? Are you home?" I bounded up the stairs and let out a sigh when she called from her bedroom. Rounding the corner, I blinked at the scene before me.

My suitcase lay on her bed with my clothes spilling out of it. Mom stood with a pair of my jeans in her hand. Tears streamed down her face.

A lump of emotions pressed into my throat. "Mom? What's going on?" Terror filled me. We were going to have to run away all because of me. "Tell me what's going on."

"Zoey, you're in danger." My mom flopped down on the edge of her bed. "It's taken all of my magic to keep you safe, but they've found you. I-I can't do it anymore."

"They?"

She put her face in her hands. The room was suddenly too hot, stifling even. I felt sick to my stomach, but I rushed over to her, wrapping my arms around her.

"It'll be okay, Mom," I said. "We can move. I'll try harder not to use my powers. You work too long at that stupid restaurant anyway. How about transferring to Florida and we can go to the beach every day? We can open a business together making surfboards."

Her little laugh tore at my heart, and she patted my arm. "It's too dangerous now. They will find you no matter how far we run. I can't protect you anymore. You need to go where you'll be safe, right now before it's too late."

I eased back. "I don't understand. What are you talking abo—"

A male cleared his throat from the hallway and my hands sparked as I leapt to my feet, raising my palms.

And the warlock strolled into my mom's room, joining us.

"How did you get in here," I growled.

"You need to listen to your mom, Zoey."

I froze, a million questions zooming through my mind faster than the subway. *How does he know where I live? Why is he even here?*

"Have you been stalking me?" I asked, not sure if I should be appalled or flattered. "What's going on? Do you two know each other?" I stared between them. My skin prickling all over. In seventeen years, I hadn't run into another magic-user. It was just me and Mom after my dad's accident.

What if he was some long-lost cousin of mine, not from the council? And I'd thought about kissing him. Really needed to get a boyfriend if my hormones were chasing down family members now. But that would explain how he was able to disappear earlier.

"Go with Reed," my mom whispered, wiping at her eyes.

Reed, so that's his name. Kinda cute, I thought, then I cringed. *Nope, the name sucks all the way to the moon.*

"With Reed? No way. Where would we go anyway?" I sniffed, blinking back tears. "What will happen to you? Is his magic that powerful?"

"Not just mine." His voice drew my attention to him. "Two others will join us at the academy where you will hone your craft and be protected."

I stiffened. "What are you talking about?"

"There's a school for magic users to the south." My mom

cleared her throat. "You'll be safe."

"Why am I just now hearing about this place?" I stood, a feeling like my mother wasn't telling me everything slide underneath my skin like an itch. "What are you not telling me?"

Her gaze flicked to Reed. "Your father sacrificed himself to strengthen the barrier around you. For thirteen years, it kept you hidden from others who would use your powers for evil. Who would turn you to the darkness."

"You sound like a character from *Star Wars*." I choked on a forced laugh and shook my head, unable to wrap my mind around all of this. "No. I'm not going. We've been fine on our own for this long. I can protect myself."

"Not anymore." Reed shook his head.

"Fuck you! I've been doing fine until you showed up." I lifted my chin, curling my fingers against the magic that burned across my palms and wanted to strike out at him. "I'm not going! Not now, not ever. So go back and tell whoever wanted to recruit me to jump out of a plane. I'm not going to your stupid academy!"

Before either of them could protest, I stomped to my room and slammed the door, throwing myself across my bed. I didn't want to go to some crummy magical school that hadn't given a shit about me or my mom for all this time. It wasn't fair that she was making me do this. Had she sent Reed to spy on me? Figured I'd slip up and use my magic at school then be able to ship me off like some unwanted child to a boarding school or something?

A knock sounded on my door and I sat up, my chin jutting out.

My mom entered and sat beside me on the bed. Like she always had done whenever we had to have a serious talk.

"Zoey, I know this is hard for you, but you can't stay."

"Why?" My voice cracked. "I'm sorry for what happened at school today, I'll do better."

"It's not just that." She clasped my hand in hers. The lines in her hand making her look older, frailer. "Your magic is maturing, like you. It's too dangerous for you and others around you to keep you in among the humans. I should have had you transferred last year, but I was selfish. I didn't want to let go of you then. I still don't."

The rush of despair hit into me like a sledgehammer. "I don't want to go. Please don't make me."

She looked away and sorrow dug a hole in my heart. "There are other witches who want to use your magic as a tool for evil. I can't hold them off any longer."

"What are you talking about?" For so long, I thought it was primarily she and I. She'd never spoke of other witches before.

Reed rapped his knuckles on the doorframe drawing our attention. "If you stay, you're not only putting yourself in danger, but your mom too."

As much as I didn't want him to be right, to wipe that look of satisfaction off his face, he was right. My mom wouldn't force me to do this if I refused. And my magic didn't always do what I wanted it to. There was no guarantee if things stayed the same that I'd be able to keep her safe or myself. I could figure out my own shit, but I wasn't willing to lose my mom too. Not after everything. Staying though, put her in danger and that was something I'd never willingly do.

I clamped my eyes shut, wanting to hold onto my life as I knew it for one more second. Not wanting to leave everything I loved behind. I opened my eyes to find them both watching me like I was a ticking bomb. And maybe I was.

"Fine. I'll go." The words scraped my throat raw. "But as soon as I learn to control my power and shove it down the evil witch's throat, I'm coming back and living my life how I want."

Mom's shaky sigh twisted my heart. She really thought this was best.

She pulled me into a hug, kissing both cheeks. "Go with my blessings. Remember how much I love you—no matter your— blood."

"What's that supposed to mean?" I drew back.

"We have to go." Reed gently pulled at my elbow. "Now."

"Wait. I need more time." I wasn't ready. Didn't know if I'd ever be ready.

My whole life, my future, everything was spiraling out of control.

Chapter 3

"Once you're settled and it's safe, then we'll talk more," my mother's voice cracked, and she missed a breath. "Make sure you wear clean socks."

A choke of laughter erupted from me and I wiped my tears. "Always."

She gave me a stiff nod. "Go, Zoey, be safe, remember all I tried to teach you."

Why did she suddenly sound like she wasn't my mom but some kind of weird mentor? Was it her way of letting go? Still, I didn't question, the words burning in my chest as I hugged her back.

"We need to go," Reed said, gently.

I let him lead me away, feeling sorrow so sharp in my heart I thought I was going to keel over from the pain of it. My mom gave me a short wave, but I couldn't tell if she was crying from my tears streaming down my face.

Outside, a small black car was parked. Reed opened the trunk and threw my suitcases inside. Normally I would've yelled that there might be something breakable inside. Lucky for him there wasn't anything except clothes and books. Instead, I stood there like a robot, unable to speak or move, until he opened the door and led me inside.

A sandy-haired blond guy was already in the back with his leg hiked over the other and wearing jeans with slashes along the legs and a faded Heavy Metal T-shirt of some band I'd never heard of. The skull and snake coming out of its mouth clued me in on what type of music.

Reed climbed into the passenger seat in front of me. The driver had dark hair and eyes from what I could tell from the back of his head and the rearview mirror.

"Sorry you had to meet Reed first, he's a stickler for rules. I'm Jasper and that's Kento." He held up bunny ears behind the driver. "He thinks he's the leader of our group."

"I *am* the leader," his thick Asian-accented voice vibrated through the car. "And I can see what you are doing, Jasper."

Jasper stopped, but not without first flicking him the finger and flashing me a smile. "So we got the damsel in distress, we gonna go now?"

"Hey, I was perfectly fine on my own." I crossed my arms over my chest, pressing my lips together before I said more than I wanted. *Damsel indeed.*

"Oh?" Reed said from the seat in front of me. "And if wraiths had shown up or a dark warlock? Then what?"

"Bet I could give the baddies a showdown…" *If my magic didn't go berserk as it often liked to do. Like blowing a hole in the school wall today.*

My mom had been teaching me magic and spells since I accidentally set the kitchen on fire when I was three and had tried to help cook dinner. Whenever she used her power, things went smoothly. With me, it was almost a toss of a coin as to whether it was gonna be good or end up with me covered in shit.

Maybe this magical academy would help me. Teach me to control my abilities, be able to trust in them instead of cringing as I waited for the outcome. Then I could protect myself and Mom— she wouldn't need to be afraid for me anymore.

"Have any questions about the school?" Jasper waggled his eyebrows. "I know all the best spots for hanging out and professors. You don't wanna get stuck with Grimy."

I couldn't resist. "Who's Grimy?"

"A freaking leprechaun who hates the fact everyone is taller than him." Jasper's leg brushed mine, and his easy smile had the corners of my mouth twitching.

"Or maybe it's the fact that you stuffed his shoes with shaving cream," Reed said.

We took the road to the freeway and I slouched down in the seat, still not wanting to go to this academy and trying to show interest in their stories when all I wanted was the world to open up and swallow me.

"Or how about when you glued his mouse to his desk or put black shoe polish on his glasses?" Reed continued.

"Now you're just bragging on me." Jasper puffed out his chest.

"Save your tricks for the academy," Kento merged with traffic. "We've got to deliver Zoey safely to the Headmistress in less than two hours."

Deliver me? Like I'm a bag of groceries? I fought the urge to say something, but what would it benefit? I was here because I had to be. Because my mom was in danger and couldn't protect me. I stilled. My body suddenly went ice-cold. Exactly who or what was after me? And would mere students and a building be able to stop them?

I stared out the window as we stopped on a long driveway that circled an ancient-looking building with stone archways and some kind of vine creeping up the sides. The place reminded me of a huge cathedral. Abandoned with dark windows and no outside lighting as the sun faded behind us.

"Welcome to Magical Guardian Academy," Jasper intoned in a mock announcer voice. "Home of the Arcane. Where the unknowable is studied and mastered."

What did I really know about these guys? Reed could've done some magical bonding on my mom or something to make her think I had to come with them, but what if it was a trick? I didn't even know why I was here except that my mom's life was in danger if I stayed. What if they'd brought me here to do some sick ritual and kill me?

My power pulsed along my hand and I clenched my fists. If they tried anything, I'd fry them or blast a hole in them like I did the wall at school.

Jasper peeked his head into the open door, and I realized I was the only one still in the car.

"You gonna stay in the car all night? I'll protect you from the leprechaun, he's not as bad as I let on."

I shook my head, swallowing against the tightness in my throat. The humidity hit me as I stepped out of the car. "Where is everyone?"

"Inside." Reed held out his hand, but I didn't take his offering.

Until I knew this place wasn't a death trap, I wasn't going to show any weakness or release my magic that was locked and loaded.

Reed shrugged, remaining at my side. Kento led while Jasper plucked at the leaves of the vines as we crossed the threshold of the black iron gate. We followed a cobblestone path to the academy's wooden gate that looked large enough for a giant to pass through. Just who all did they have at this school?

A cool wind tickled my dark hair as the door swung open. Flickers of lights from candles lit stone walls. Gold rugs with purple, blue, and red swirls laid across the floor. A vaulted ceiling rose up above us, also in the same grey stones used throughout the place.

"This way to the Headmistress' office," Kento said without even glancing back to see if I was keeping up.

Was he anxious to deliver me and wipe his hands clean? I finally spotted a few students in school uniforms, so unless they planned on attacking me for my power or killing me, I was safe.

We entered a small office with an oak table and a woman sitting behind it with folders and papers in neat stacks on her desk. Her gray hair was pulled into a tight bun and I could imagine her with a ruler in her hand and rapping students' knuckles who didn't obey.

"Ms. Zoey Dane," she adjusted her rhinestone glasses. "Congratulations, Reed, for finding and bringing her in."

He bowed his head. If I hadn't done magic at school and in front of humans, would he have known? Yes, Mom had said this was necessary. Being here would protect me somehow and keep her safe. That was all that mattered. She was the only family I had in this world.

"I'm Headmistress Olsen." She gave me a tight smile. "Before you are admitted into the academy, you must pass several tests."

"What?" I looked between the three guys who kept their gazes from me, except for Kento who met my stare unblinking.

"Why?"

"We can't just allow anyone into our facility." She straightened her navy blazer. "And since you've never been formally trained and at your age, you must pass with near-perfect scores."

Shit. Why had my mom made me come here? But if I didn't pass, then what? They'd send me back? Part of me debated not trying on purpose. They'd kick me out and I'd be back with Mom. Then I remembered the look of terror on her face when I had suggested us moving.

Someone or something was after me and she wouldn't be safe if I returned. Not until I worked out who the hell wanted me dead.

Chapter 4

"Reed will show you to your room." Headmistress Olsen slightly bowed her head. "Testing will begin at eight a.m. tomorrow, so I suggest you settle in and get some rest."

I followed Reed, Jasper and Kento out of her office, my heart, feeling like a dead weight, sat in my chest. How was I going to pass magical quizzes? Seriously doubted they were multiple-choice ones. Half the time, my magic was on the fritz on a good day. I couldn't count on it. Not to fail me or arc into something else. I was so screwed.

Numbly, I climbed the stairs after Reed with Jasper beside me and Kento taking the back.

At the third floor, Kento cleared his throat. "Your room is at the end of the hall. Don't be out without an escort after sunset."

"Why?" I forced a smile. "Are there vampire mages?"

His face contorted into a scowl, then he took the next flight of stairs without answering.

"Hey, I was kidding." I faced Jasper and Reed. "There isn't any such thing as vampires, right?" Just dark mages that used blood magic and other forbidden acts to enhance their powers.

"Be sure and get plenty of rest," Reed said in a clipped

voice. "Breakfast is at seven sharp. Once the food is gone, you won't get anything else until lunch, after your first two examinations."

Unease sank into my gut. Just how many chances for me to fail were there? What if I didn't make the cut to stay here and learn? I had to. Mom was counting on me and I wanted to be able to protect us. To be able to live on my own without others bossing me around.

"What's for breakfast? There aren't magically made foods like eggs and bacon?" I kidded. Not really caring if I had any or not as long as there was extra crispy bacon and orange juice.

Before I could say anything else though, he continued. "Don't be late. That will strike off points from your overall score."

Jasper set down my suitcases he had been carrying. "Dude, you're freaking her out. It's her first time here."

"Would you rather I lie to her?" Reed snapped back. "Tell her that all of her troubles are over?"

"They aren't?" I asked, half-joking.

Reed shot me a look that had bile rising into the back of my throat.

"Not every witch or mage is invited to the academy. Those who are, must prove their worth."

"Can't be too hard." I waved a hand, pushing aside my nervousness. "You three got in."

"This isn't a joke, Zoey." Reed tensed. "There's been a war

going on since before you were born between good and evil. We hope that you've got what it takes to stand up for what's right. Though, we've never accepted anyone already set in their ways and as old as you before."

"Well, you brought me here, remember?" I crossed my arms. "I never asked to come here."

"Pickings have been slim lately." The muscle in his jaw twitched as he clenched his teeth.

"How about I have a little practice by frying your ass like I did to the wall at school?"

"Pranks here aren't rewarded." He glared down at me, but I refused to back up. "Neither is showing off. Though I doubt you could take me."

"Yeah?" I puffed up.

"Look, I get it. Yesterday your life was fine, now it's all screwed up." He sighed. "Try to lose a little bit of that hot temper out on the field tomorrow. You're going to need it."

He strode away.

"Wait, I'm not done talking to you." I had a million questions about the testing. Was there a cliff sheet I could cram for? A stress headache clamped down on the back of my skull.

But Reed was already out of earshot.

Jasper turned away too, giving a low whistle under his breath.

"Um…can you tell me about the testing?" I asked,

hopefully, my nerves starting to eat me up inside. Not to mention, Reed had been right. I missed my old life and my mom already.

"Sorry, no can do. That would be cheating."

"Hey, will I have a roommate?" I asked to lighten the mood, but more out of curiosity than anything. I'd been an only child my whole life. Might be cool to have another girl to lounge with.

"After you pass the first week of testing, you may get assigned a roomie, but right now you've got the place to yourself."

"Oh," I said, sounding a bit more disappointed than I meant to. First week?

"Take Reed's advice." Jasper gave me a sad smile. "Crossing fingers that you pass."

"Thanks." My throat suddenly felt dry.

Jasper disappeared and I was left alone.

I dragged my suitcase into a dorm room with two small beds, a nightstand between them, and a bathroom and two closets. The beds were bare, with stark white mattresses on iron frames. Nothing fancy. Almost was like a half-step up from a prison cell.

I opened the closet and found sheets and a thin blanket. First thing I was going to do if I got accepted into this place was to buy some proper bed sheets, comforter, and a dozen decorations. Somehow, I had to turn this dreary room into a bedroom I wouldn't cringe to see every day. Plus I wouldn't feel so homesick if that was possible. I've never been away from my mom before— she hadn't even allowed me to have any sleepovers.

Rolling back my shoulders, I focused on making up the bed. All I had to do was get through this. However, in order to do that, I needed to pass these tests. But that thought had my insides cramping up, which made me want to forget this whole thing and run away.

My thoughts drifted to Reed, Jasper, and Kento. The desire to prove them wrong had me wanting to defeat them now. No one knew more or anything about what I could do.

Where was he and this stupid school when I was trying to control my magic? On top of that, the Headmistress had congratulated him for bringing me in, like I was some kind of prize.

Anger still twisted inside me at having no choice but to come here, but I didn't have any other options right now if I wanted my mom safe. Plus seeing three arrogant wizards with their mouths hanging open while I blew these tests sky-high was going to be so worth it.

Chapter 5

The next morning, I took a quick shower, brushed my teeth, then pulled my hair up in a ponytail. Since I had no idea what today's magic testing would entail, it was best to get my hair out of my face.

I hadn't unpacked yet. Something about putting all my belongings in the small dresser in the dorm room made everything feel more real. Besides, I didn't want to jinx myself by believing I could sail through whatever quizzes they had at this academy. If I unpacked, I'd have the added jab of having to stuff everything back into my suitcases when they told me to leave.

A huff escaped me as I opened the heavy door that groaned across the thick carpet. If my mom wouldn't have been in danger if I had decided to stay with her, I'd have given Reed the finger and told him to shove his academy's charms right up his arrogant ass.

I trailed down the hallway. The dorm appeared so different in the daylight. Ancient with stone walls with tapestries of gold, silver and purple.

Finding no evidence of an elevator, I took the stairs down into the main lobby. They creaked with every other step. The black banisters of carved wood felt like history under my hand as I trailed my fingers down the railing.

Nerves danced inside at having to prove myself with my magic and not knowing if I had enough control to be accepted. I'm worried about my mom and if she is truly better off without me there, as well as fitting in with kids who had probably been raised eating, sleeping, and breathing magic where I'd only a few magic lessons that I had to beg my mom for. Her philosophy had been that too much magical knowledge led to corruption. Most of my spells I'd done on trial and error. Mostly error.

I followed a group of students to the cafeteria and snagged a tray with flimsy bacon and eggs that looked too yellow to be real. A piece of toast smeared with butter completed the ensemble and looked the least revolting of the entire breakfast.

"Ready for test day?" Jasper pulled up next to me, his tray overloaded with nearly burnt bacon.

"Hey, how did you get crispy bacon like that?" I asked, frowning from my floppy piece to his perfect dozen.

His sandy-blond hair needed a haircut, but it swept to the side, accenting his bright hazel eyes. He waggled his eyebrows. "Because I'm so devilishly handsome, I get special treatment from the cook. She puts mine on first and doesn't take it off the burner until I arrive." He picked up a piece, snapping off the end. "I've got the timing down to a science."

I swiped a piece of crispy bacon off his plate and popped it into my mouth and moaned, closing my eyes. Cooked to crisp excellence, bringing out the smoky flavor. I opened my eyes to find him staring and my face heated. "What?"

"I can forgive you for stealing my bacon if you keep making sounds like that."

"Whatever." I rolled my eyes at him.

"Ready for today?" Reed dropped his tray in front of us. "Better eat up, don't want to hurl out on the field."

And there went my good mood. "Don't you have something better to do than gawk at me?"

"Nah." He smirked, snatching my limp piece of bacon from my plate.

"Hey, that's mine." I reached across the table and grabbed it back.

"You were already drooling over Jasper's burnt bacon." Reed bit into my food. "I could tell you were going to let this poor guy feel abandoned."

I crossed my arms, leaning back. "It needs to be crispy, not raw."

"And I suppose you cook all your meat until it's blackened?" He arched an eyebrow.

Reed didn't know me. No one here did and for them to pretend they did, irked me. "No, I like my steaks medium with a little pink."

"I like some things pink too." Jasper pushed a piece of his bacon toward me.

My skin heated at his innuendo. Maybe this place wouldn't be as bad as I'd feared.

Reed narrowed his eyes, glancing between us. "What's the cost of burnt bacon these days?"

I didn't answer him but shrugged a shoulder as I chewed on the scrumptious bacon. Let him think whatever he wanted. Served him right for stealing my food and giving me a hard time.

Kento strolled over to us with a protein shake the color of a fluorescent shamrock. "So this is the popular table today?"

"Which kind of bacon eater are you?" I waved my hand at the two extremes in front and beside me.

He lifted his glass. "Vegetarian, so neither."

Jasper made a gagging sound, then oinked before he stuffed more bacon in his mouth. While Reed poked at his eggs like he was hunting for lost treasure.

"Are there actual veggies in there?" I asked. "It looks like you blended all the green marshmallows from a cereal box."

He shook his head. "No, this is a powdered protein mix, almond milk, and some fruits and spinach. You should do this every morning to cleanse your body and your magic."

I made a face. "Maybe next time."

Did he think there was something wrong with my magic ability? I clenched my hands as my magic itched across my palms. *Not here, not here.* I'd get expelled if I let loose in the cafeteria.

"See? Your aura is cloudy, and your temper is flaring,"

Kento lectured me and unease sank in my gut.

He made me feel like I didn't belong here. Like I was fooling myself and maybe I was. Maybe all of this was a mistake and they'd see during the testing that I was way out of my league. That my magic wasn't something I could control most of the time, but a wild beast that bucked and had to be beaten into submission constantly. The magic zapped up my arms and I winced, breathing deeply to try and calm down.

"Get it together," Reed snapped.

"Easier said than done." I pushed aside my tray, suddenly having lost my appetite.

Twenty minutes later, a professor dressed in black leather pants and tight-fitting athletic shirt stood at the front of the cafeteria with a megaphone. Her hair was pulled into a tight bun. "All new students and exchange students from North Haven and Luna Academy meet out on the soccer field."

I stood along with eight other students.

"Good luck." Jasper swallowed his food.

Even Reed gave me a curt nod. Kento sauntered off and spoke with the headmistress who glanced my way.

Talk about nerves. I squeezed my hands into fists, locking them at my side as I followed the group of testers outside. I hadn't been this worried since I had landed the role of Rapunzel in middle school after the lead vomited all over the tower half an hour before the show started. The entire time, I died under that thick, blond wig with the smell of puke and cleaner wafting in the cardboard cutout.

"The quickest way through the test is to use your instincts," the vampire slayer looking teacher said. "Just hope they are the right ones."

"What are the wrong ones?" A guy next to me raised his hand after he asked the question.

"Dark magics. Blood magic—anything of that sort will get you immediately disqualified."

I knew what blood magic was, obviously, but what classified as dark? Not that I thought I did anything opposite of white and pure—there were just some heavily gray areas too— right?

"Each of you will take a turn putting a wraith back into the underworld."

Holy fuck! I thought day one testing would be simple, like changing water to wine or making Brussel sprouts taste like cotton candy. Turn our hair blond or something, not put a spirit back into the bellows of hell.

"Zoey?" Reed asked, suddenly at my side.

I hadn't realized I stopped moving as soon as I found out what the test was. Fifty feet from me stood a cluster of eight other students surrounding a creature that resembled a grim reaper minus the scythe and just as menacing.

Gritting my teeth, I faced him. "A wraith? Are you guys nuts?"

"It's what everyone has to pass the firs—"

"How many tests are there?" I straightened my spine, locking my arms at my sides so I didn't punch him or accidentally hurl a ball of magic at him, not that he didn't deserve it. "Wait, Headmistress Olsen said a week's worth of testing? So what's Friday's assignment? We gonna raise an army of zombies and see if we can banish them before they destroy the world?"

He snatched my arm and I ignored the tingles that spread from his touch. "Keep your voice down. Do you know how many students the academy turns away? This is a chance of a lifetime."

I glanced away, unable to look at him right at that moment. Headmistress Olsen watched from a stone balcony. Her face drawn down into a scowl and I remembered her congratulating Reed on finding me.

"No." I jerked from his grip. "This isn't about me at all, is it? Or the academy, it's about your pride and winning kudos with Olsen. I'm just a pawn piece that you happened to capture, and it'll tarnish your record if I fail."

The muscle in his jaw twitched and his arctic blue eyes darkened. His magic pulsed in the air between us like thunder about to boom. "It has everything to do with the academy. You're in magic school, Zoey. What did you think you were going to learn? How to weave a cloaking spell or mix a love potion or practice tarot?"

I lifted my chin. "Well, yeah."

"I thought you wanted to learn real magic. How to protect yourself and your mom after graduation."

"And?" I still didn't understand. "What has that got to do with battling a magic spirit creature on the first freaking day? Shouldn't that be like a mid-term assignment?"

One of the guy's in the circle around the wraith screamed as if the creature had ripped off his flesh and fear gnawed at my belly.

"Go home, Zoey. I admit that I was wrong about you."

Anger flared in my chest, white and hot. "Don't you dare walk away from me. I'm here because of you and my mom. Both of you said she'd be in danger if I stayed."

"Exactly." He rolled his shoulders back, the wind tussling his white hair. "But this is a magic guardian school. You'll need to learn to deal with much worse things than a simple wraith."

Chapter 6

"Magic Guardian Academy? What is that supposed to mean?" I asked, daring for a little bit of pride to swell. "Like we're witch cops?"

Reed's mouth twisted into a smirk, and I pushed aside how it made my heart beat faster in response. "We ensure that the world, both magical and human, are safe. But all this is too much for you if a simple wraith scares you."

His mockery had me burning up on the inside.

"I'm not scared." I stuck out my chin and marched toward the students clustered around the black, cloaked figure. But inside I was quivering, unsure I could do this, but still, I called over my shoulder, "Piece of cake."

Two older students carried out an unconscious student who had a bloody arm and his eyes were as wide as Frisbees. I swallowed down the terror that squeezed my chest. What was I thinking? This was way out of my league. I only had experience with bullies…human ones.

Wraith. Okay, what did I know about these things? They were creatures of the underworld who craved flesh and drove people mad if they were able to possess them.

So no touching the thing.

Check.

I didn't even want to get near it, but I took my place in the opening the failed guy had vacated. A coldness seeped into my bones like I'd suddenly opened a deep freezer. At least they were having us do this as a group and not one on one.

"Travis, you're next," the professor called, her voice echoing.

My stomach plummeted into my shoes. *Shit! So much for all of us taking it all at once.*

A boy with spiked green hair grinned, showing off more like it. "Been putting these bastards down since I was five." He lifted a hand, closing his eyes and muttered, "Redi, nec amplius noceat."

The wraith shrieked, and I covered my ears from the sound, wincing. Its black cloak whipped in an invisible wind. Inside its hood was an empty blackness. A hollow. It floated like a ghost and seemed more phantom than physical except for its skeletal arms and hands that occasionally peeked in and out of the cloak's long sleeves.

"Redi, nec amplius noceat," he shouted the words again, high-pitched this time.

I glanced at him, his face was pale, and all the earlier confidence was gone. *Oh fucking crap, this is going to go bad.* He had no control.

Travis strangled out a cry, his eyes bulging.

"Help!" one of the girls screamed.

"Prohibere, prohibere," the teacher yelled, clapping her hands and magic shot forward into the wraith.

But the creature didn't flinch or anything. Not even a teacher could put this thing back where it came from. The wraith struck out its boney hands and power crashed into me, zapping along the circle like a live, exposed wire. I fell on my knees as did the other eight students around me. If we didn't get the creature back to the underworld, if it got out...it could kill dozens of people before dusk.

The wraith hissed, flying toward us so fast that we scrambled backward.

I ducked my head as another uncontrolled blast of magic zipped over my head. Sweat drenched me as fear clutched my throat, squeezing. I stood on shaky legs. Somehow, I had to put this monster down.

My magic sparked across my hands as I gathered up the power, aiming it at the creature. Instead of dodging or moving back, it merely crooked its boney finger at me. I tossed out the spell, the magic ripping from me like a heavy weight, and it sank into the creature, making its dull, black robes seem to glimmer.

Fuck!

Around me, everyone's faces paled, but they started spewing out spells so fast I couldn't make them out.

Magic zigzagged around the small circle. A pop sounded in

my ears and one of the girls was lashed backward. Wind churned around us forming a vortex.

Shit!

"Zoey, don't!" Reed's body crashed into mine at the same time my spell unleashed and sizzled over our heads. It crashed into a car in the school's parking lot several feet away. The entire vehicle blew apart. "It's feeding on your magic."

"How do you know that?" I yelled. I hadn't given my spell that much juice.

Reed grabbed my hand and yanked me to my feet. "Stay behind me."

"But I—"

"Do you even know how to expel a wraith?"

"No," I admitted, my throat dry. How were we going to beat this thing? "If throwing magical energy at it isn't the answer, any other ideas?"

"Yeah, don't die."

The wraith in the middle of this chaos cackled like this was the funniest sitcom he'd ever seen. It stretched out its skeletal hand to the boy who'd cast the spell. Magic flared forward, striking the guy in the chest. He crumpled face down into the dirt.

Oh shit, oh shit. Is he dead?

Another girl screamed as her body went flying along with the first one. Dirt, leaves, and two more bodies sailed along in a tight circle around us. The air snatched out of my lungs as I opened my mouth to attempt a counter spell.

"Præcipio tibi in profundum inferni." Reed tossed a glowing silver ball at the being who just sucked it into its body like a black hole.

None of the magic was working!

"I will feast on all of your flesh," the wraith shouted against the wind, laughing. "Unleash the dark powers with the dark mage's child."

Another scream echoed in my ears. This one was from a guy who was bent backward. Some wayward spell threatened to break his back.

Suddenly, the power yanked me from the ground like a giant fist. I choked out a breath as my ribs constricted. I couldn't breathe.

"I will taste your flesh first," the wraith's voice echoed as it floated closer.

"Zoey!" Before he could take a step, Reed was thrown backward into one of the poles of the football goal. He groaned. Blood coated the side of his face.

No! I thrashed, tried to get free to help him. But the invisible grip only tightened. I fought for air as spots danced before my vision. "I banish y—"

I couldn't get any more words to come out. My power sizzled across my palms then flickered out. The wraith's black hood shown its void-like face inside as red glowing eyes stared down at me…into my very soul. Terror snaked down my spine. I stared at death.

"Taste the darkness," the wraith's voice rumbled inside my skull.

The edges of my vision dimmed as I gasped, trying to draw in breath, but only finding a vacuum that sucked my soul out bit by bit. I gritted my teeth. Tried to fight. Muscles growing weaker. *Oh god, I'm gonna die.*

Sounds around me faded. The wraith's skeletal hand reached out. My body jerked. Starved for oxygen. Tears streamed down my face as I fought once more. Fought to finish the spell. Fought for my life. Colors around me spun into grays and blacks while the icy hands of the wraith stroked my cheek.

I convulsed as my body hung in the air within the creature's grasp.

Cries sounded in the distance. They seemed so far. It felt like the wraith had taken slivers of my soul and only a fragment remained. Flares of magic from others burst at the corners of my vision but neither the wraith nor the vortex it had created stopped.

I tried to scream, choking on blood as it filled my mouth.

My vision dimmed. Sorrow slammed into me that I'd failed. My first test. My first freaking day here at the academy. Failed my mom.

A rumbling vibrated around me, pulsing the air, matching each slow beat of my heart.

The creature flinched back. Power flared inside my chest hard and fast.

What the hell?

Searing pain rushed forward, bowing me back. Heat surged throughout every cell of my being. I screamed without sound. I was being burned alive from the inside out.

Then the magic blasted out of me with a boom like a bomb. The wraith exploded into tiny fragments of black ash that floated harmlessly to the grass. I collapsed onto the ground, coughing out blood, gasping in the air that stung my lungs.

Students who had been locked in the tornado dropped around me, choking and coughing. Two hugged each other. Others cried. Blood was splattered on their faces and clothes. Teachers and spectators on the edge of the field muttered, pointing at me as they raced toward us. Self-conscious, I ran a trembling hand over my dark hair and made sure I still had clothes on.

"How did you do that?" Travis asked with a shaky voice.

"I-I..." I wasn't sure how to respond because I had no idea how my magic had ricochet out of me like that. Everyone stared at me, judging me, but I didn't want to be a freak. Not here, not among those who were supposed to be my own kind.

"Thanks," Travis said in a hoarse voice. "I thought I was a goner!"

So had I.

Chapter 7

Reed! I checked the dwindling crowd for him as other students passed by, giving me double-takes. Some smiled, others had a pinch to the edges of their eyes or mouths. They all judged me, but I never said I had complete control of my powers. And who in their right mind sets a wraith against first-year students?

Where the hell was he? My heart thumped hard against my chest as I searched the grounds, past the students moving in every direction—there—he was slumped over with an ice pack he held onto the back of his head.

I dashed over to him, wanting to check on him to ensure he was all right. He had tried to shield me from the wraith. I owed him. When he glanced my way, I slowed my pace, stopping a foot from him, suddenly self-conscious.

"Hey, isn't there a spell or something for that?" I asked, trying to hide the way he made me nervous.

He winced. "Nah. Sometimes magic isn't the answer to every problem."

"Right." I bit my lip, looking back over the field where a black stain marred the perfectly cut green grass and where the wraith had been. "Um…thanks for, you know, trying to save my life."

"Seems like you did just fine on your own." He leaned against the metal football goal with its orange paint chipping off, keeping the ice pack in place with one hand. "Thought you said you didn't know how to take down a wraith?"

"I didn't—don't." God, admitting the truth might get me expelled. But what if the next test I faced something much harder and people were hurt worse than this time. This time we'd been lucky. And I'd no idea how my magic had done that. "I mean…I don't know all the fancy magical words like you guys do."

"What was it that it said to you?" He frowned. "When it touched you?"

"Nothing." I shuddered, not wanting to remember the icy-cold feeling that had taken my breath. That had made me taste death like ashes on my tongue. How the wraith seemed to see into my soul and the choking blackness.

"It didn't attack you directly…not like the others. Why?"

"No idea." I shrugged a shoulder. "Why did the magic spells to bind and banish it not work?"

"Are you sure it didn't say anything?" He glowered. "It looked like it did while it was absorbing your magic or something."

I tensed, thinking I was seconds away from death when it had absorbed my power until somehow my magic backfired on its ass. "What did that look like to you?"

He nodded like my answer made sense to him. "Threads of your magic were being unwoven and sucked into the wraith. It was glowing this obsidian black color. Dark as night and shining. And the vortex around it...no one could get through to help you. How did you destroy it when it had been taking your power? You shouldn't have had anything left to do that kind of damage."

"Kinda been winging stuff my entire life." I shifted from foot to foot, hoping he didn't ask for more information, because I had no idea how I'd blown the wraith to ashes.

"Don't say that shit too loud." He glanced around us quickly, then returned his attention to me with a frown. "You want to have your powers removed?"

"Wha—why would they do that? I thought I was here to learn."

"If they think you could go rogue...that your power is too volatile and a danger... Then they'll remove the threat."

How could I have been so stupid? A lashing pain hit my middle at the thought, and I wrapped my arms around myself. I couldn't live like that...no magic...like a regular human. That would be the worst thing that they could do to me. Sweat broke out across my forehead, my insides quaking. And how could I be so dumb and tell Reed that? Now he held that knowledge and could hold it over me.

"Right." He stood and started walking toward the school, tossing the bag of ice into a trashcan as he passed it and I jogged to keep up with him.

"So what's the next challenge?" I asked. Secretly hoping it would be something simple like taming a griffin or lassoing a dragon.

A young girl ran up to us. "Headmistress Olsen wants to speak with you." Her red hair was braided into pigtails tied with ribbons that matched the plaid of her school uniform skirt.

"Tell her I'm on my way." Reed took the stairs two at a time.

"Not you," the girl said, "her."

I freaked. "What does she want?" My throat went dry. Had Olsen figured out that I had no idea what I was doing, and my magic was unpredictable? What if she took my power? I wouldn't be me anymore. Magic had always been a part of my life. It would like to be living without my soul. Void and dead inside.

"How should I know?" She smacked her gum. "I'm just the messenger."

With my heart thumping harder than ever before, I followed the girl to the Headmistress' office.

"Thank you, Lacey," Olsen said in a stern voice from her desk.

The door clicked closed behind Lacey and I sat in one of the visitor's chairs with sweat rolling down my back. Olsen's mahogany desk was loaded with files and magic books like she'd recently been searching for something.

I straightened in my chair, rubbing my hands on my thighs. What if she asked me questions about the wraith and I answered them wrong? Then she'd realize that I knew nothing of fancy spells and magical language. I'd reveal the truth that I didn't belong here. That my magic was a wildcard and maybe too dangerous for me to keep. I clenched my hands in my lap.

What did it matter how I got rid of the wraith? Olsen had said *flying colors* and damned if blowing a wraith to smithereens didn't qualify for that. She should want to move me to honors classes or something. But Reed's tense expression when I told him I winged my magic popped into my mind and my shoulders tightened.

"Miss Dane." She steepled her fingers, looking over them at me. "We have strict rules at this school. Magic must be controlled, contained." She clasped her hands on the desk on top of a folder. "The wraith got out of control because you allowed it to feed on your power."

"I-no. I did no such thing." Dread plunged in my gut. God, she was going to take away my magic. "I was trying to stop it. Banish it like we were instructed."

"And yet, you didn't utter one word of a spell to do so."

My face burned in a mixture of resentment and humiliation. "I was never taught the language of spells. But no one else was able to do anything—not even the teacher on the field."

"Enough." She slammed her hand down on the desk and I

jumped. "You will learn the proper ways of handling and using magic. I cannot have you continue to test until you at least know some basic spellwork."

I slumped in my seat. Returning home would endanger my mom. Not to mention she'd be so disappointed in me that I couldn't even cut it the first day. But how could I stop the Headmistress evicting me from the school in disgrace? If I could stay here, learn what I could, then I could protect her, and everything would be the way it used to. I needed this education. I needed to be able to face things like a wraith and know that I could do what I did. I just had to figure out how I'd done it in the first place.

"Please, I'll try harder, don't expel me."

"No. I don't think that's the answer either." She huffed. "You will have three weeks to learn spellwork including basic magical words to bind and banish. Then we'll have your second round of testing."

I opened my mouth to say thank you, but she continued.

"If you show progress at that time, we will consider allowing you to stay. Keep in mind, though that our students study for years before they master the basics. I'm afraid you'll have your work cut out for you. And I've arranged for the best tutors to help. It will all come down to your focus and hard work, though."

Her message was clear. This was my last chance to even have another go at their insane testing otherwise not only was I out, but I would also be mundane. My future depended on me being able to cram years' worth of study into mere days. I swallowed the lump of anxiety pressing into my throat. I reached my hand out to shake hers. "Thank you. I promise you won't regret this."

She stared at my offering, but didn't take it, so I stepped back and lowered my arm. "See that you don't."

Chapter 8

When she opened a file, her eyes lowered, I guessed I was dismissed so I slipped out of her office.

My heart rose up into my throat. How was I going to learn everything required to take down monsters like the wraith in mere days? My luck, there wouldn't be any cliff notes or crash course to learning the proper banishing ways of stuck-up magic users.

I bit the inside of my cheek as I went down the hallway toward the library. Why hadn't Mom shown me all of this? Or at least let me come here and borrow magical tomes to read over. Get myself familiar with my power. But I'd had to learn on my own most of my life. Mom would get anxious whenever I asked her a direct question about magic. She only taught me enough not to harm myself, because she knew I'd never stop trying to figure out how to use my ability. Now that I was here, I wished I'd pushed her more to teach me.

"Where are you going?" Jasper leaned against one of the marble columns with an unlit match sticking out of the corner of his mouth.

My breath caught and I skidded to a stop. "Library. Gotta do some major cramming."

"Nah, that place is just full of dusty books." He pushed off from the wall and grasped my hand, tugging me along with him. "Only thing you could get in there is a headache from all those words."

I tugged against his hold, stopping in the middle of the hallway. A cluster of students weaved around us, some throwing uneasy looks over their shoulder. Wow, rumors must spread fast in this school. Why else would their faces appear like I would strike them if I got too close.

"Why aren't you coming?" Jasper pushed back his sandy hair, switching the match to the other side of his mouth and I wondered what tricks his tongue could do.

I shook my head to clear it of the lustful musings. "Do you want me to fail? I've got to study."

"That's what we're going to do. Trust me." He winked and sauntered away like he was sure I was staring at him.

At the cockiness of his walk, his broad shoulders, his tight ass. My feet started moving of their own accord because he was right. I'd rather be with him...the library could wait.

"Wait up." I jogged after him. What would one afternoon of goofing off with Jasper hurt? Had to be better than eyestrain and I could pick his brain on his magical experience. Gleam some tips and practice a few magical words.

We pushed out the double oak doors and into the early afternoon sunlight. I blinked, adjusting to the brightness. The academy was a huge, refurbished mission, had limited lighting. It looked permanently evening time inside no matter what time of day it seemed.

I inhaled the fresh air, missing my mom and how we'd eat outside every Sunday unless it was raining. She'd gotten a picnic basket on her wedding day from my grandmother as a family tradition. She and Dad ate cheese and crackers with a bottle of champagne after they got married because they'd been so excited, they'd forgotten to eat beforehand. When I was born, they continued. And even after Dad died, we kept having our Sunday afternoon picnics.

At the thought of my dad, my stomach clenched. Mom had said he died protecting me. But in racing to get out of the house, I hadn't had time to have her elaborate. I needed to check on her. Let her know I'd passed the first test—even if it was with a restriction. If I called her, she'd hear the underlying panic in my voice.

"You coming?" Jasper called out ahead of me.

"Yeah." I took out my cellphone and texted my mom while I followed him.

Hey, Mom, I passed the first testing. Gotta study for the next one. Call you later. Love and miss you, Zoey.

I hit send and bumped into Jasper's back. "Sorry."

"This where it happened?" he asked, his voice low and in awe rather than the smirking of earlier.

I glanced past him to where he was talking about and bile rose in the back of my throat. He'd taken us out to the football field, right beside the black, inky stain four-foot-wide where the wraith had been earlier.

"Is this some kind of joke? Cause it's not funny." I turned away from him. Shit, I'd been so stupid to think he'd help me. He just wanted to find out about me blasting the creature for whatever morbid reason.

"Hey, hey." He dashed in front of me blocking my path. "It's not like that at all."

"Oh?" I stared up at him, ignoring the pain in my chest at allowing him to trick me like this. "Then how is it?"

"First, you need to trust me." He held out a hand.

I looked past him to the blackened, flattened grass. Logic told me to run back inside and pour over books. But the slow smile he gave me made my heart speed up. I sighed, "What the hell."

"Yes!"

"But if this doesn't help me, I'm putting a spell on you to have all your hair fall out or something."

He squirmed but moved back to the spot and knelt. "Come closer, but don't touch any of the black area."

"Why not?" I sat beside him.

"You don't want to resurrect a wraith, do you?"

"Gez, then why the hell are we here?" I went to back away, but he grasped my hand.

"Relax. This is a safe zone for the next thirteen hours. No magic done here can harm anyone."

After the trouble, I had with the last one, no thanks. "How do I know you're not making that up?"

"It hurts me that you don't trust me." He placed a hand to his chest.

"Sorry, but I don't really know you."

"Fair enough. Guess you'll have to wait and see. In the meantime," he took the match out of his mouth, "Concentrate on this red tip here. Focus on it until it is all you see."

I narrowed my eyes, trying to do what he said.

"Tell me when you've got the tip as the only thing in your vision."

"I'm working on it." How long was this supposed to take? I scratched my cheek.

"Stop fidgeting," he chuckled, "God, you're worse than me."

"Is that supposed to be one of those backhanded compliments?"

"Maybe." His voice was light and playful. "Be a good girl and keep practicing and you may get a prize from the teacher."

"Promises, promises." I smiled, but when he tapped the match to my nose, I glared at him.

"You're not trying hard enough."

"You do it then." I huffed, leaning back on my hand.

"No." He shook his head. "I already learned how to do this when I was five."

"Show off." I sighed when he held out the match again. "Fine."

Sitting back up, I forced my eyes to stay on the stupid little match tip. Why couldn't he have given me something larger? "This is impossible."

"Feel yourself sinking into the match. Into the fragments of the red, unburnt parts, the potential here much like your own."

"Isn't there a shortcut to this? Like a magical spell to make this easier?" I kept staring at the match, wishing he'd say the exercise was done.

"Sure, there are ways around everything, but then the next step will be harder, and you'll want to cheat. And the next and the next until your soul is as empty and dark as the wraith was."

"Wow, I didn't know you could channel Reed. You sound just like him."

"Reed has his points. Don't agree with him on everything, but on this, I do."

"Why?" I blinked, my concentration breaking.

"Personal experience."

The air around us shifted, making the hairs on my arms stand up. "You can tell me," I prodded.

"Let's just say dark magic is very seductive. Now. The match."

"Ugh, I'm never going to get this. Can't we do something fun?"

He gave me a crooked smile. "Sure, I can think of a lot more things I could be doing with you right now."

My heart skipped a beat at his sexy tone and the way his grey eyes darkened with promise.

"But first, you've got to light this."

Rolling back my shoulders, I refocused as he held up the tiny wooden stick. I ground my back teeth, wishing the damn thing would hurry up and strike so I could enjoy my day and hang out with Jasper. This time I felt myself sinking into the tip. The scene around me, outside of the match, blurring. "Done."

"Right. Now imagine a single filament of the match igniting."

"No." I didn't look away, even though sweat trickled down my back. "I'll set you on fire."

"Not if you do as I say."

Fear clung to me like a strangling vine. "It's too risky. I-I don't have control over my magic like you do."

"I know how to extinguish myself."

"I can't—" My stomach heaved.

"Do it!"

Before I could look away, a popped sounded. The match held a flickering flame.

"Holy cow, I did it!" I let out a laugh not believing it was that easy.

"Told ya." He grinned and extinguished the flame.

Behind us, a girl screamed. I whirled, dreading what I would see, knowing that it was going to be mega bad.

Her sweater was on fire!

Chapter 9

I don't even remember standing up, but suddenly my feet were pounding across the ground to reach the girl on fire. Someone had thrown a jacket over her to squelch the flames, but it didn't do any good and the magic had the jack bursting into flames too.

Shit!

"Zoey, stop," Jasper huffed as he ran behind me.

The girl was going to be burned alive if I didn't do something. Her screams scraped the air.

"In flammas exstinguere," someone shouted. But the flames rose higher as did the girl's shrill pitched screaming.

Heat poured off her like an oven set at the highest temperature. When I reached out to touch her, my skin blistered and I hissed out a breath, jerking my hand back.

She collapsed on the ground, her dark eyes pleading with me as her skin blackened before me.

My gut seized and I pushed down the acid scalding the back of my throat. I could do this. Had to do this. It was my fault the magic ricocheted.

Her screams turned into hoarse cries. I sank to my knees beside her and grasped her arm with both of my hands. The searing pain shot up my arms. I ground my teeth, refusing to let go. Flames chewing along my flesh. Like I'd done with Jasper and the match, I imagined the opposite. The flame growing smaller... snuffing out. Gasps echoed around me, but I dared not open my eyes. The heat still was intense like sitting inside a bonfire. I let out a breath, imagining blowing out birthday candles.

A cool breeze whipped around me and took more of the heat.

Sobbing hit my senses and I opened my eyes. The girl trembled under my touch. Ash covered her and her skin was blistered red. The magical fire was gone though.

I pulled back. "I'm so sorry," I whispered.

"Megan," a teacher rushed up to us, "What happened?"

"I-I didn't mean to." I swallowed the lump swelling in my throat. This was going to get me kicked out of the academy for good.

"You did this?" She narrowed her eyes at me.

"It wasn't Zoey." Jasper stepped forward. "I'm responsible. A simple fire spell went askew. I don't know how... we were in a safe zone."

I couldn't let him take the blame for this. "No, it was me. My spell backfired somehow."

"Here, I'll give you a spell to numb the pain and put you to sleep temporarily so we can get you inside to the nurse." The teacher whispered words over Megan. The girl was hunched over, whimpering. "Then we'll figure out what happened."

Megan's eyes fluttered closed and her body floated over the ground as the teacher gently led her into the academy.

An aching pain hit my hands and arms. They were blistered all over and some spots were charred black. But I had fared better than Megan. She had the same as me but over half her face, her entire torso and both arms. I couldn't even imagine the agony she was going through.

Remorse slammed into my chest as I followed the teacher and Megan inside, Jasper trailing behind us.

Mom had said that I needed to come to the school because if I stayed, she'd be in danger. That the school would teach me how to protect myself. What if that's not exactly what she meant? What if she meant that I was the danger? That if I stayed, I'd end up doing this accidentally to her or worse?

Inside the school, the nurse chanted healing spells over Megan. Except they barely improved. She tsked, flipping through a book that much have had a thousand pages in it.

"Why isn't it working?" Megan croaked in a raspy voice. "This is all her fault."

"Just need to find the right spell." The nurse turned the pages faster.

My gut twisted with anxiety. What if Megan was permanently this way? Scared because of me? "Is there anything I can do?"

"I think you've done enough," the nurse snapped, and sorrow struck me so hard that I couldn't take in a deep enough breath.

I hadn't meant for this to happen. A simple spell that probably anyone could do here since they were a child. And I'd fucked it up and hurt someone in the process. I clenched my fists, not caring that my nails dug into my palms.

"What about borrowed magic?" Jasper asked from the corner of the room.

"How do you mean?" the nurse glared at him. "Dark magic? No, I won't condone that in this school for whatever reason."

"But if black magic can heal her?" I interjected. "Then how is it bad?"

"It's more gray magic than black." Jasper pushed off the wall with his foot. "Not as pure as white but not as evil as black. A mix."

"And still just as dangerous." The nurse slammed the book closed. "Nothing is working on her injuries."

I glanced from her to Jasper. "So what's involved?"

"Nothing too major." Jasper gave me a crooked smile, but it didn't reach his eyes. Those were pinched at the corners like this was a bigger deal than he was letting on. "A little bit of blood, from both of you and some of your power."

"What does that mean?" Megan hunched further on the nurse's exam table.

"It means you both will feel like you've run a triathlon and will probably sleep for several days." Jasper shrugged. "But when you wake up, you'll be healed minus a few scars that Nurse Jenkins will be able to reduce down until they're almost invisible."

"Yes." I stood. "Let's do it."

"No freaking way. She's a walking curse!" Megan gasped, closing her eyes as a wave of pain hit her and my stomach clenched. "Oh god, it hurts so much."

"But if it'll fix your injuries?" I offered. "I-I didn't mean for this happen. I'd do anything to heal—"

"I don't want anything from you." Megan glared at me. "I don't want to be tied to you or owe you a damn thing."

"Megan," Jasper said softly, "it was an accident and my fault. Zoey was just doing the spell like I asked her."

Tears rolled down her cheeks, but she lowered her eyes and gave a nod. I imagined if she didn't have the numbing spell earlier, she'd be in so much agony that she wouldn't even be able to speak much less even hear us over the pain. And all this was my fault, no matter what Jasper said, it was my magic that had lashed out and attacked her. Whatever I could do to make it up to her I would, even if that meant taking her injuries and pain into myself.

"There's one more thing." The nurse tapped her foot.

"Doing this ritual will bind you and Megan together."

"Like twins or something?" I had always wanted a sister, but not this way.

"Fuck, I don't want to have anything to do with her." Megan crossed her arms over her stomach, then scrunched up her face as a wave of pain struck her and my throat closed up.

"No, like doppelgängers." The nurse shook her head. "On an astral level, you'll be each other, so to speak. Closer than twins. An exact copy."

"Meaning…" I frowned.

"That if something happens to one of you, the other will feel it." Jasper cleared his throat.

"He means if one of us dies," Megan's mouth twisted in disgust. "Then the other will experience the death like her own."

"No way." I backed up, fear clawing up my throat. "There's got to be something else we can do."

"I've tried everything." The nurse wiped a hand over her face. "But we won't do this unless you both agree."

This wasn't my choice, it was Megan's. She'd been the one the most hurt. I could live with scared up arms. I straightened. "If she wants to do this, then I agree."

Megan smiled at the burnt part of her face pulled up tight. "Yes."

"Then let's get started. The sooner the better with these types of spells to reverse the damage." Nurse Jenkins opened a first aid kit and pulled out a silver-looking dagger. "Zoey, you first."

I held out my hand and winced when the blade sliced across my palm leaving a throbbing sting in its wake. Then she did the same thing with Megan's palm. Jenkins let our blood collect in a small vial. Then she shook it up, dividing it into two flasks.

"Drink. Each of you."

I downed the blood mixture in one gulp. The metallic taste clung to my tongue anyway.

"Now, repeat after me," Jenkins said. "Colligabit vulnera sanant duae. Sicut superius et inferius."

"What does that mean?" I asked. If I was going to start learning a magical language, I needed to figure out what the words were.

"Bind these two and heal their wounds," Jasper answered. "As above, so below."

I nodded then stumbled over the words while Megan said them perfectly exactly like Nurse Jenkins had.

My magic snapped through me, bowing my back. Pain lashed across my skin like something was attacking me. Clawing at my flesh and trying to rip my bones from my body. The room spun as my scream tore from my throat and darkness shrouded everything.

Chapter 10

I woke up with a groan, feeling like my body suddenly weighed five hundred tons. Light danced behind my eyes, but I yanked the pillow I was laying on over my head. Did I have the King Kong flu? Cause it felt like a giant mound was sitting on my chest.

"So I take it you're not a morning person," Jasper said.

"Hmmph," I mumbled into the pillow.

"You need to eat, Zoey."

Everything about the other day rushed forward. Megan's screams echoing, the replay of her on fire and her blackened, scorched flesh afterward replied over and over. My stomach heaved. "Can't. I'll be sick."

He disappeared into the bathroom and I realized I wasn't in my room as there were posters of motorcycles and a Ferrari with a blond on the hood hung on one wall. On the other side of the room was shelves of books, neatly stacked and organized by color, and a collection of swords. Two pairs of men's shoes were placed on the floor in front of a bed that didn't have crease or wrinkle in the bedspread.

Jasper returned, handing me a wet washcloth. A thrill raced

up my spine when our fingers touched.

"Where am I?" I wiped my face with the cool cloth.

"My room—well, mine and Kento's."

I stiffened, thinking I hadn't even checked if I still wore clothes, and lifted the bedsheets. Yes, I was still in my school uniform. If I'd been undressed or worse, naked, Jasper and Kento were going to get slapped.

I tossed the covers off me and sat up.

"How are you feeling?" Jasper laid a hand on my bare knee.

The answer stuck in my throat as all I could focus on was his hand on me and the warm tingles spreading up my body. I was suddenly tongue-tied, not able to form words.

He brushed my hair out of my face. "I've been worried. You slept for two days."

"What about Megan?" I swallowed my suddenly dry throat. The bond between us felt like a wet blanket across my back, but it didn't tell me if she was healed or not. God, I hoped she was okay. Even if she hated me, I could live with that, had enough people disliking me because I'd always been a loner. "Did the spell work?"

"She's going to be okay." His gaze softened.

I let out a breath. "I was so worried about her. God, Jasper, did you see what I did to her?"

"It was an accident, Zoey. No one blames you."

"You sure about that? I would if I was Megan. What if the

fire had killed her? Or left her permanently scarred?" I shivered. "I don't belong here, Jasper. I'm screwing everything up worse than I did back home."

"Hey." He leaned forward, his hand cupping my cheek. "So the spell got out of hand, I shouldn't have pushed you. It's my fault—I should've ensured there was no one else around but us."

I met his stare. "And what if I'd done that to you? I'm a horrible person and an even worse witch."

"No, you're not. Just untrained." His thumb stroked my cheek and I lifted my hand to cover his.

My breath hitched as I swore he was staring at my mouth. He shifted closer, glancing from my eyes back to my lips. He moved his hand up a fraction and I let out a small gasp from the sharp tingles spreading through me.

I wanted him to kiss me more than I wanted to breathe. To forget all my problems, everything. Just experience this intimacy with him. To take away the pain of what had happened that gnawed at me.

He glanced up from underneath those thick lashes with a smoldering look that I couldn't take it for another moment. The anticipation of his kiss burning me up inside.

He lowered his mouth to mine and fireworks shot off in my head.

His lips grazed mine and my body eased against him. At that moment, I didn't want to be anywhere else. All of the tension from everything quickly faded. He kissed me softly at first. His tongue skimmed across the seam of my lips, and my heart thumped. I opened my mouth, tasting him, gripping his shoulders as I held on as the waves of pleasure built up inside me.

Our mouths and tongues exploring one another. His hands on me felt so right.

A gust of wind and a door slam had me blinking in surprise. Trying to focus on what just happened.

"I leave you alone for five minutes and you two are sucking face?" Kento seethed.

Mortified, I scrambled off of Jasper's lap. He didn't look the least bit embarrassed only annoyed that we'd been interrupted.

"Zoey, get dressed," Kento snapped. "You're with me the rest of the day to work on your magic properly."

Stiffly, he walked to the window, clasped his hands behind his back while he waited.

Jasper blew me a kiss. My face burning, I dashed to the bathroom to take a cold shower. I hadn't even been here a week and already I'd made a mess of things and nearly screwed a guy I barely met. Yup, couldn't wait for my date with Kento the drill sergeant.

Chapter 11

Underneath my heartbeat, I felt Megan's presence. It was like an echo. I pushed aside the thought of her hating me because of what I did and dressed in record time, quickly braiding my damp hair. I was going to carry the weight of what I did for the rest of my life.

Jasper had gone to my room and brought back a change of clothes for me. Since it was Saturday, I didn't have to wear the school uniform and my jeans never felt more amazing. When I exited Jasper and Kento's bathroom, Reed was standing next to the bed waiting for me.

"Where's Kento?" I asked.

"He and Jasper are chatting, so you're with me till then."

His tone suggested he knew everything about the kiss.

Despite my face burning, I straightened and marched toward the door. "Then I'm grabbing some of Jasper's extra-crispy bacon while we wait."

"Don't you care about what happened? How your magic leapt to someone and caused so much damage?"

I spun, noting his clenched jaw and fists at his sides. "Do you think I did this on purpose? That's why I'm here, isn't it? To learn how to control my magic and use it the *right* way. Although I'm not sure after yesterday, I'm not even sure if I'm capable of anything close."

"Zoey," His tone was harsh. "We need to deal with this. Figure out where your magic went wrong and fix it so it doesn't happen again."

When he grasped my arm to stop me from going, his fingers were warm and sent a shiver through me.

"Sure. When you rip my magic from me." I pulled out of his grasp. "No, thanks. I'll hit the books and try to do this my way. We've seen what happens when I work with one of you."

I wrenched the door open and strode out. All three of them should be whipped. They'd been going to this school probably their whole lives and as seniors, they should have known better. I was a wild card and regular rules didn't apply to me.

A bitter chuckle erupted from my lips. Coming here, I'd been semi-hopeful that they could help me learn to protect myself. Never thought I'd be classified as a rogue. Not fitting in here just like back at my own school.

I bypassed the cafeteria, the thought of eating made me feel nauseous. Students still wearing their pajamas rubbed the sleep from their eyes as they shuffled toward the cafeteria for breakfast. Most were probably sleeping back in their beds, but since breakfast stopped at nine, these stragglers wanted to grab something before all the food was gone.

Jagged rain hit against the roof and windows, making the morning look dreary and dull. Lightning flashed followed by a boom. The building vibrated from the impact and the chandeliers swung from the arched ceilings.

In the lounge area, I sank into a plush blue chair and leaned over the edge to view outside. The window faced the football field. The black spot where the wraith had been was painfully visible despite the overcast skies.

I shifted to move to a different chair when a shadow zipped out of the blackened grass. My breath caught. Was that the wraith? Had it come back? I broke out in a cold sweat.

Another figure darted from the blackness about the size of a wolf. *Oh, fuck!*

Boom! I jumped with the thunder crash. Two more wolves slunk out of the black spot. Terror pierced me.

I glanced around, but nobody else showed any kind of alarm. Dread sank into my chest and I stood on wobbly legs. Whatever these things were, they'd come from where the wraith had died, and all my instincts said the creatures were dangerous. That they weren't mere wolves.

"Hey, there are things—wolves that just came out of the ground," I said running up to a group of students.

One balked and the others shook their heads.

"Enough of the drama queen stuff, we get you're powerful, but stay away from us," a boy glared at me.

"Yeah, none of us want to end up crispy like you did to Megan."

I clenched my fists, rage and regret burrowing into my heart. "That was an accident. You have to listen to me—I think the school—that we're in danger. I saw wolves emerge from the ground and—"

"Stop making things up."

Not waiting for anyone else to spot the half dozen wolves stalking the school, I ran down the hallway to Olsen's office.

"Zoey, wait," Reed called out.

"Can't." I didn't stop even when he kept pace alongside me. Everything in me screamed that danger had come. I had to find a teacher or Olsen.

"Wait, we need to talk." Reed grabbed my arm, stopping me. "Why are you in such a hurry? We fucked up. I admit it, but—"

"There a wolves outside of the campus."

He blinked, shaking his head slightly like he thought his misheard me. "Well, yeah, the woods line the edge of the academy on the west side."

"No. From where the wraith was struck." I waved a hand. "They crawled out of the blackened circle."

He paled. "How many?"

"Six...Eight? I stopped counting and came to tell Olsen. What are they?"

"Native Americans call them Wendigo. They're cannibalistic and feed on human flesh." He started running toward Olsen's office, and I went after him. "The wolf is their first form—soon they'll turn into werewolf-like creatures—able to walk to two legs. And immune to most magic."

"Wonderful," I said sarcastically.

Lighting cracked, followed closely behind thunder that made the lights go dark.

A scream echoed back toward the cafeteria and I froze. Part of me wanting to race to try and help and the other terrified to take another step.

Olsen burst out of her office, drawing short when she saw us. "What's going on?"

"Wendigos, we think."

She clasped a hand to her chest. "Get Zoey to safety."

Behind her, Jasper and Kento skidded to a stop at seeing us.

With a nod behind her, she continued, "All three of you use whatever magic you can to protect her."

"Wait, what?" I asked. "No, I want to help fight. What about the other students, don't they need protection too?"

"Let us handle this, Zoey." Olsen lowered her hand and marched forward. "We know what we're doing."

And just like that, the barb of her words jabbed me in the gut. She didn't want my help, none of them did. I watched her run down the hall in her high heels shouting orders.

I turned to Kento, Jasper, and Reed. "This is because of me, isn't it? From what happened to the wraith and it wasn't banished properly?"

Jasper glanced down at the floor, his feet shuffling back and forth. While Kento gave me a look of pity. The muscle in Reed's jaw twitched.

They didn't need to answer my questions. The truth was written all over their faces.

Chapter 12

"It's not what you think," Reed said, his gaze full of pity.

I arched an eyebrow at him, waiting for his reply, but he didn't continue. We both knew that I screwed up with the wraith and burned Megan. Even though it was on accident, it proved that I had no idea what I was doing, but I wasn't willing to give up despite the fear gnawing at my insides. "So how do we defeat these Wendigos?"

"You're not going anywhere near them," Kento nearly growled.

"Hey." Jasper jogged up to us. "Zoey, this isn't practice in a controlled environment like the wraith."

"Yeah, cause we saw how well that turned out." I sucked at basics. What would fighting Wendigo do to my magic? What if blew up the whole school? But I couldn't stand by and do nothing despite the terror squeezing my chest.

"So what do I need to know?" I asked. "You said the Wendigos are immune to most magics. I'm guessing fire is out?"

"Most definitely," Kento answered behind me. "As is electric or binding spells."

"And air and most water ones too," Jasper added.

"You know, you guys don't have to come." I turned the corner and found it empty of monsters or students. "In fact, it might be safer if you were nowhere near me. Maybe we should evacuate the whole school." That way if my magic backfired, no one would be around to catch the whiplash.

"And how are we supposed to protect you if we leave you alone?" Kento shook his head. "We are honor-bound to keep you safe."

"What about the other students?" I paused at a cross-section, straining to hear anything to know which direction to take. Fear raking up my throat.

"They have their own bodyguards or are equipped enough to take care of themselves."

Shrieks sounded to our left.

"You sure about that?" I bound toward the screams. Then a pain struck my leg and I tumbled forward. *What the fu—Megan.* My astral twin was being attacked. I was feeling her pain. No way could I do nothing now. I owed her more than my terror. "We gotta go!"

I pushed up to my feet and charged forward, ignoring the lancing pain in my calf.

At a juncture, we continued left and I stopped at the sight in front of me. Several students lay bleeding on the linoleum. Wolf-like beasts chomped on legs and arms. One had Megan pinned beneath its paws, its jaws locked around her leg.

"Rigescunt indutae," Kento shouted.

One of the animals snarled, its ruby-red eyes narrowing. It lunged at us.

"Try something else!" I grabbed a plaster bust of some old guy on a stand and hurled the piece at the wolf. The head smashed next to the animal but didn't faze it. It crept forward, head low as it watched for threats.

"Aquae vulneribus," Reed tossed out, his magic looking like a wave of water that tunneled at the wolf. It pushed him back but three of his buddies surged forward.

Jasper grabbed the stand the marble head was on and jabbed the underside of iron legs at the creatures. "Any better ideas?"

I bit my lip, wanting to try, but freaked that I would screw this up. I noticed black liquid on one of the wolves' snouts. Was that blood? The guys had said they were only immune to some water spells. What about the water…blood in their veins?

But I didn't know the damn magic language that everyone around here flashed like privileged badges. My gaze met Megan's. She said volumes in her eyes without saying a word. Out of everyone, she knew that my magic could backfire, hurt more people than the monsters here. To save everyone though, she was willing to take that risk.

I'd never had anyone believe in me as she showed me in that one-second, even if it was begrudgingly, and it floored me.

My hands rose as a power swelled in my chest. *Please don't mess this up. Please work.* Inside I felt sick.

I imagined the blood in their veins slowing down. Coagulating. Turning sluggish as it slowly stopped. The creatures howled and snarled. All of the coming toward me now. My arms trembled as I tried to hold the spell. If I could just keep them a few moments longer, I was sure it would kill them.

"How are you doing that?" a girl next to Megan asked and she shushed her.

Sweat trickled down my back. My arms shaking so bad I could barely keep them lifted. Jasper and Kento rushed up to me, each holding up one of my arms.

"Take our magic, use it along with yours," Jasper said.

"Wha—" I furrowed my brow. "I don't know how to do that."

He gave me one of his winning smiles that set my heart aflutter. "Sex magic is one way."

A bark of laughter burst from my lips. Leave it to Jasper to be a goof in a time like this.

"We don't have time for jokes." Reed picked up the stand that Jasper had been using. "Siphon their energy, their magic, from where they are touching you and use it to power your spell."

"Won't I drain them too much?" I whispered, my voice going hoarse as I was losing the energy to even talk. My legs tried to buckle but Jasper and Kento held me upright. If it wasn't for them, I'd have fallen down.

"Isn't that black magic?" If I couldn't do basic, white magic right, what would happen if I used the opposite side of the spectrum? An iciness snapped over my heart. "No, I can't…it's too dangerous. Someone will get hurt. I can't risk it."

The Wendigos yelped but their bodies morphed, growing huge, turning into werewolves. Their mouths looked like they could crunch a person's head off in one bite.

I trembled. The desire to run filled me so hard and fast that I took a stumbling step backward. It was only Jasper and Kento's hands on my arms that kept me from bolting.

"We don't have time," Reed shouted as he broke half the stand into one of the monsters' heads. "Do it now or we're all dead!"

I closed my eyes focusing on the warmth of both Jasper and Kento's hands on my arms. Trying to ignore the panic swelling in my chest. How both of them held me up. The way Jasper and I had kissed earlier. How Kento looked so sexy when he was jealous and had wanted to spend time with me and I wanted to get to know him too. How Reed had tried to protect me from the wraith and even now was fighting off giant werewolf creatures.

Howls broke out to our right. I dared a glance and my heart slammed against my chest. Half a dozen more wolf-creatures were running toward us. I looped the magic spell-like gathering wool and tossed it at them too. But it was weak. It only slowed their pace, it didn't stop them like the first group. Snarls and yips sounded behind us as four more Wedigos stalked toward us.

It was too many. Why had I thought I could even tempt this? I had no idea what I was doing. I'd failed twice before using my magic here. "I-I can't hold them all."

"Take my energy. Take it all." Reed threw the broken stand at the oncoming wolves who darted around it, then he placed both of his hands on either side of my face.

Before I could grasp what he was doing, his lips lightly brushed onto mine.

"Whoa, dude! Not the time for that," Jasper grumbled.

Kento tightened his hold on me and waves of magic washed over me. Threatening to drown me. Reed pressed his body to mine, his kiss filling me and easing the ragging currents inside me, while Jasper and Kento held my arms up. Their energy shoved forward with mine, each of theirs vying for dominance, for power. Turning my world upside down.

I was going to die. Turned inside out from all this power. It was too much. I shook my head, trying to pull away, but Reed's hands on my face kept me in place.

A burning sensation started up each arm then ignited in my chest. I screamed out a gasp as Reed, Kento and Jasper fell unconscious at my feet.

Unlimited power raced through my veins. I felt like a goddess. That nothing could touch me. Nothing could hurt me. That I wasn't a failure, but was for the first time in my life, all that

I was supposed to be. Like I had been made for this. That all the magic I'd dabbled in before was a crutch. This was what I was supposed to be. Magic.

One of the wolves leapt at me, and I flicked a hand at it. Blood splattered across the academy's window as its body was rent into two pieces, guts hanging out everywhere.

Another wolf lunched and I did the same to it and another. The Wendigos quivered, some falling dead where they stood as the last of my spell to turn their blood solid, manifested in a flash.

The remaining crouched low, backing up, looking for an escape. But I would give them none. I would tear every last one of them to bloody pulps.

Chapter 13

"Zoey." Headmistress Olsen crept forward with her hands out in supplication. "You've done enough. Return the magic to Jasper, Kento, and Reed."

My mind couldn't wrap the meaning around her words. What was she talking about? All this power was mine. I squeezed my hands and two more Wendigos imploded. It felt like I squished a grape in each palm. "No one could stop them except me."

"That's the darkness talking." She took a step toward me. "You mustn't listen to the seduction of it, it's not real. It's stolen."

"No." I shook my head, her words confusing me. "I-I borrowed…t-they gave it to me."

"Yes, to fight the Wendigos, but look…there are no more. We're safe."

I blinked and the dozens of wolf-creatures I'd been fighting laid in blood heaps with their insides strewn all over the walls and floor. My stomach heaved.

"Let the magic go that's not yours." She stopped when I glared at her. "It will return to the rightful owners."

"With this power, I wouldn't need anyone. I could protect myself." And my mom. We'd be safe. I wouldn't need this damn school with all its rules and snobbery and me feeling like a bum that couldn't do anything in their presence. Now they feared me. Now I was in charge and they had to listen.

I lifted my hand toward her, and her eyes bulged. The smell of her fear was like a sweet dessert that I wanted to gobble up.

"You see?" Megan sneered. "I told you she was a dark mage. She stole their magic and is attacking Headmistress Olsen."

I blinked, trying to clear my mind of her words. Her loathing for me raking against my heart from our bond.

"She's keeping their magic, she's killing them."

"No." I shook my head. Guilt squeezing my chest. I didn't want to hurt anyone. Hadn't meant to harm her. It was an accident. I wasn't evil. The sound of Megan's screams and whimpers replayed over and over in my mind. No, I wasn't evil. Acid burned the back of my throat and I wanted to push away the pain.

"She tried to kill me too." Megan glanced around her at the other students who either nodded in agreement or took a step closer as if to defend her. "You saw how her magic burned me."

My magic rumbled inside me, demanding to be let out and teach everyone here that I was the best. That I was superior to them all. Yet, a deeper part of me wanted peace, wanted friends, wanted acceptance. Inside, I felt like I was being ripped in half. Tears stinging my eyes as I struggled to maintain my grip on the intoxicating magic that promised everyone would bow at my feet.

I shifted my gaze to the three guys who lay around me and

my heart twisted so hard in my chest that for a moment I thought Olsen had sent a hex at me. I ground my teeth, the power I held was so intoxicating that I couldn't let go. Didn't want to.

"Vro—" Olsen started saying a spell and I clamped her mouth shut by pointing a finger at her.

This new power throbbed within me. But there was a hint of more…of ley lines that pulsed near the school. One of which was where the wraith had exploded, and the Wendigo had come out of. It called to me. Whispered like whenever I was nearly asleep and thought someone called my name.

More than anything, I wanted to prove Megan wrong. That I wasn't a bad witch.

I stared at her, part of me about to dismiss her and let my power do whatever it wanted, when one of her tears slid down the partially healed scar on her face. The one that I had put there by fooling around with magic that I didn't understand. That I really had no control. That the power surging in my veins and making me feel invincible, wasn't mine.

"H-How do I stop this?" I croaked out and bent down to brush Jasper's hair out of his eyes and touch Kento to ensure myself that he was okay. The memory of Reed's kiss was still on my lips.

"Imagine the power seeping out of you and into them," Olsen said, rubbing her throat, but her voice was kinder than I thought it would've been considering I had essentially cursed her.

I nodded, closing my eyes and trying to picture what she said.

"I'll help you."

Opening my eyes, I found Olsen kneeling in front of me. I licked my dry lips, praying this worked and brought back Jasper, Kento and Reed. I wanted to see their smiles and hear their banter and jokes. Wanted to kiss Jasper and Reed more. Hell, I wanted to know what kind of kisser Kento was as well.

They were three parts of my life that had fit so snuggly in such a short time, but I couldn't imagine a world without them.

Magic leaked out of me like someone drained all the blood out of my body but a few drops that kept me alive, leaving behind exhaustion and a hollowness that ached to be full again like I was before.

Color came back into their faces and joy filled my heart. I stifled my smile when they opened their eyes and sat up.

"What happened?" Reed asked.

"I just saved all your asses, that's what," I smirked. God, it felt so good to have done something positive without aftermath.

"Fucking hell," Jasper coughed. "I feel like I've been dragged by a truck for twenty miles across rocks."

Kento bowed his head at me. "You did amazing. Just as I knew you would."

"Kinda my fault we were all in jeopardy."

"How do you figure?" Jasper asked.

"The Wendigos, they came from where the wraith was exploded and the ley line out there." I turned to Olsen. "Which is dangerous doing magic so near there, isn't it?"

"Yes, well you've taken care of the threat." She stood, straightening her jacket. "I think you've earned another chance at the school. You'll begin classes in the morning."

My mouth hung open. "Just like that, I'm in?"

"Not quite." She patted the back of her hair as though to ensure her bun was still secure. "A trial period. But we'll continue with your testing at the agreed-upon time."

Bummer. Now I had classes and a deadline hanging over my head.

"And since you've connected with these three Seniors." Her gaze swept up Jasper, Kento, and Reed. "They will be your escorts and ensure your safety."

I tensed. "What do you mean, my safety? The entire school was attacked by the Wendigos." Did she think that the other students would blame me and start bullying me or something? "I can take care of myself."

"That remains to be proven." Her features softened and she gestured me away from the chaos of the injured students, Nurse Jenkins who swooped in to help them, and others picking through the Wendigos' bloody mess.

"Did you see anything," she asked, "before the Wendigos appeared?"

This was it. She thought it was a random thing. "I saw them rise out of the blackened earth where the wraith had been exploded." There went my chance to attend the academy. She'd retract her statement about allowing me to go to classes and kick me to the curb. Couldn't say that I blamed her. I'd do the same.

She frowned. "Nothing else?"

"No. Except for the storm that came about the same time they appeared. Look, I'm sorry my magic did this and brought these creatures here. I never meant for anyone to get hurt." *Unless they deserved it.* A small voice in my head said.

"Wha—no, you aren't responsible." Reed touched my arm, hesitantly. There was fear behind his eyes.

"How do you figure that? A simple match spell made—" I said.

"Made everyone realize how special you are," Jasper cut in, but even his goofy grin looked strained.

"It's a trick." Megan hissed, but gave me a lingering look. "Don't think this changes anything between us."

But before I could voice a reply, Olsen started talking, not even looking at me.

"Someone deliberately used that energy from the wraith to conjure these Wendigo. They were attacking everyone in their path to get to you, Zoey."

"No, we were stopping them from hurting others and that's why they came after me."

Olsen clasped her hand in front of her. "No, Zoey. We've been here for hundreds of years and never have had two catastrophes like this before. While the first might have been you, the second was not. It was intentional and since it was used at the sight where your magic destroyed the wraith, I'd say they were seeking you."

"Me?" I asked. "Why?" But part of me whispered it was because of the power buried inside me. The one that had blasted the Wraith. The one that sucked up all three guys' powers like a half-priced cherry slushy on a hot summer day and still wanted more.

"Told you that you were special." Jasper brushed his sandy hair out of his eyes.

Fuck. "No, I was safe until I came to this school. Would somebody please tell me what the hell is really going on here?"

Chapter 14

"There are those who practice magic who follow an evil path." Olsen adjusted her glasses.

"You mean dark mages. What about them?" Mom had been petrified of anyone practicing evil magic, which was why she was so reluctant to teach me anything. I had tasted that power. I still hungered for it even though I knew it was wrong, but the desire for it surged in my veins like I needed another fix. But I couldn't let it control me. Couldn't let it win. I clenched my fists against the growing need. I wasn't evil. No matter how much my magic seemed to want me to be. "Why are they targeting me?"

Reed cleared his throat. "They sense your magic is powerful and they want it for themselves."

Something passed over Olsen's face, but she schooled her features before I could decipher it.

"Yes, Reed is correct. Best thing we can do now is get you trained as soon as possible and have at least one of these three guarding you at all times."

"I don't need babysitters."

"This is for your protection as well as the students in this academy. I hope, Zoey," Olsen softened her voice, "that you will at least give us a chance. The same curtesy we are doing for you."

I gave her a quick nod and she rushed away to help the others. With the stress of everything resting on my shoulders, I grabbed a trash bag from a teacher handing them out and started helping to scoop in the Wendigos' remains. I couldn't help thinking though, that I'd been safer before I came to this school.

We worked the rest of the day, evening coming quickly, but I forced down the soup the teachers offered everyone.

The floors and walls were finally cleaned. Who knew that Wendigos could make such a steaming, stinky mess. It smelled like rotten fish and I blanched.

"I'm beat, I'm going to crash into bed and not wake up until Monday."

"You can't be left alone. Not after the attack and what happened." Kento's brow furrowed.

Jasper let out a low whistle. "Like sleep in her bedroom?"

I spun. They just wanted to keep an eye on me to make sure I didn't become all evil like before. "I don't think so."

"No, he's right." Reed nodded and my mouth dropped open. "But it shouldn't be Jasper to guard you. It should be me."

"Absolutely not." I lifted my chin. "That has to be against all the school rules—I can't have a guy in my room after hours."

Reed cocked an eyebrow. "We'd sleep outside your room. Close enough for you to call for help if needed. We could magically tie your emotions to whoever was guarding you in case someone tried to hurt you from inside your room and we didn't know. You need to be safe, Zoey."

"That's not the point." Plus, I didn't really want any of them around me while I was sleeping. What if they snored all night?

"Unless you have a better idea, I will be staying with you tonight." Reed gave me a strange look I couldn't quite read.

"Not really." My shoulders slumped slightly. I was beyond tired and didn't want to argue any more. "Fine. But you are not to come into my room under any circumstance unless invited."

His grin made images of letting him in flash through my mind and made my whole body heat up.

Monday morning, I donned the academy's uniform, while my stomach did summersaults. I snuck past Reed out into the hallway who was asleep on the cot. I didn't need to wake him up for permission to go to class. This whole idea of Olsen's having me guarded morning, noon, and night was just ridiculous. I felt like a child that couldn't fend for herself.

The weekend fled by with the whole school cleaning the hallways, mending the injured students, and consecrating the black area of the football field. If anyone didn't know that I'd exploded the wraith and my residual magic used to conjure the Wendigos, they sure as hell did now.

Mostly I got two responses. Either downright avoidance like I had the plague or envy like they debated if they could win a magical duel against me or not. Yup, the only difference so far between this and human school was the magic.

I tucked my headphones into my ears and turned the volume up on my favorite punk song as I strolled toward class. My first one was Magical Potions. And I had to admit, part of me felt a bit giddy at being able to take enchanted classes. Had to beat the hell out of Calculus class.

A hand touched my arm and I eased out one of my earbuds.

"Why didn't you wait for me?" Kento said. "I'm to escort you to your classes until after lunch."

"Because I really don't want bodyguards following me everywhere." Bad enough I had Reed staying outside my room for the past two nights. We'd both been so tired with fixing the Wendigos, consecrating the ground where they'd emerged, and putting up extra protection wards around the school that we'd fallen asleep as soon as our heads hit the pillow. But now things were settling down, what would happen this evening when we weren't tired? Nervous anticipation danced across my skin.

"Why don't any of the other students have upperclassmen shadowing them?"

He tensed, looking away with a pinched expression on his face.

"It's because of what happened to Megan, isn't it? And me

borrowing the power to defeat the Wendigos. I'm dangerous and you're not really protecting me, you're shielding the others from me." Had they known my magic was on the brink of becoming catastrophic? Is that why they'd recruited me from home so quickly and why I had a deadline looming over me?

My stomach heaved and I wrapped my arms around myself. I felt like I was going to shatter into a million pieces. The shadow of having all that power beckoned me. I didn't want to be evil. I wasn't bad. Remorse slammed into my chest and I gasped. I felt sick inside. If this academy of magic couldn't help me, who could?

He rubbed the back of his neck, still not meeting my eyes. "There's a lot more to it than that."

"But I'm right, aren't I?"

Chapter 15

I didn't wait for his answer but marched down the hallway across the Oriental rug to the Potions' class. Inside it resembled a human biology lab with small tables and two or three stools behind each. The teacher's desk was crowded with books, test tubes full of liquids I couldn't identify, and half a dozen small saucers.

All of the students gawked at me, fear evident in their expressions as I walked between the rows of tables. I took an empty seat near the back and groaned inwardly when Kento sat next to me. Wasn't that I didn't like him, just didn't I like the idea of him hovering because he'd been ordered to. Like all three of them watched me like a ticking time-bomb that would go off at any moment.

"Morning, class." A woman with long brown hair tied into a loose ponytail breezed in through the door. "Today we'll review common potion ingredients and their usage."

A girl's hand rose up in the air. "But Mrs. Powell, we went over all of that at the beginning of the year."

"Yes, well," Mrs. Powell rummaged through the books on her desk. "Never hurts to have a refresher. Mid-terms are coming up next month before winter break and will cover everything we've gone over so far."

One of the kids groaned and shot me a glare.

Wonderful. I'd traded-in humans thinking I was a freak to magical kids knowing that I was and either hated or feared me. I didn't ask for anything except being part of a group.

"Best way to remember things is to have hands-on experience," Mrs. Powell continued. "Take out your notebooks and pens. I'm going to give you all of the list of items to collect for a spell. Your job is to gather the items and then tell me what we're making."

This sounded different in a good way. I took out a piece of paper and a pencil, ready to take notes.

"Everyone will need to work in teams, doesn't matter what size."

Murmurs rose as students decided who would be in their group. No one even looked my way, but I hadn't expected them to either.

I tore the edge of my paper off and pushed it to Kento. "If you're going to babysit me, then you're going to help."

He took out a pen from his backpack, but there was a twinkle in his eyes when he thought I wasn't watching.

"You will need a basket on high, wool of bat, eye of newt, tongue of dog."

I blanched but wrote out the required items. Were we really going to cut out a newt's eye and a dog's tongue? *Gross.*

"The toe of frog, Adder's fork, wolf's milk and dragon's blood." Mrs. Powell smiled like she hadn't given us a list of animals to harm. "We'll meet back here in half an hour."

Grabbing my list, I followed the other students outside. My stomach rolling at the thought of doing all of this for a simple potions class. And where in the world were we going to find a dragon? Not that I minded being able to see a real-live one but the idea of making it bleed didn't sit well with me. Neither did the dog's tongue. It had to be code for something else.

"Why the frown?" Kento asked as he hiked beside me. "Think of this like a scavenger hunt."

"Mutilating animals is fun for you?"

"Did you even open your textbooks?" he asked.

"Kinda been busy saving the school and recovering," I quipped, glancing down at the list. "Unless these are code words for something else."

"Exactly." A twitch tugged a smile at the corners of his mouth. "So what would wool of bat mean since they have fur, not wool."

I frowned, searching around me. "Give me a hint."

"Maybe the outline of a similar shape?"

"That doesn't help me at all." I shook my head, but walked toward the forest. "A type of herb or planet doesn't narrow it down any."

We walked deeper into the forest and I purposely kept us

from getting too close to the other students as I didn't want to be called out as a cheater along with all the other bad things they believed me capable of.

I spotted a black-leaf bush. "This one? It's the same color as a bat."

"Nope. Think shape."

"Are we going to have me guessing the entire list? We'll be here all day."

"Just two of them. The rest I'll tell you, but you need to study."

"I will, I will." I waved a hand and moved deeper into the forest. Couldn't be a flower as I didn't see how that would make anyone think of a bat's wing. For a while, I walked in what felt like circles, not finding anything.

Over the hill, I spotted a tall bush with red berries. "Wait, is that Holly?"

"Yes." He beamed and my heart skipped a beat at his praise. "The nickname for holly is bat wing because of the resemblance."

Excitement filled me as we hiked to the blooming bush and tore off a few green leaves. I was finally doing something that wouldn't injure anyone, hopefully. Kento put the leaves in his pocket.

"Good job, what's next?" he asked.

"Are you always like this?"

He frowned "Like what? Precise? Dedicated?"

"I was thinking more like reserved."

"What's wrong with that?" He kicked aside a pebble on the trail.

"Nothing, if you're sixty years old." I paused, staring at his profile. "You're not, are you? I mean if you're an ancient vamp or something who can walk in daylight, I won't tell anyone."

"Wha—" He let out a chuckle. "No, I'm not a vampire."

"But you are ancient? Cursed to attend this magical academy forever?"

This time, I got a half-smile out of him. "No, I'm not old. I'm only eighteen." He shrugged. "I was just raised this way. My family was very conservative and strict. No emotions, no boasting or bragging. We all had a duty and did it without question or complaint."

"Like what?" I veered closer to his side to avoid a muddy hole as we walked.

"My chores were seeing to the family's safety, cooking twice a week and washing my own clothes. Had to be able to support myself, do for myself, while also helping out the family."

"Then why aren't you still with them?" I asked, shooing a buzzing fly.

"I went out to celebrate my thirteenth birthday." He stared off into the distance. "I thought I had become a man. Me and my friends found some rice wine in an alley and we took turns drinking it. I couldn't even walk straight once we were done and passed out. While I was gone, my little sister—she was too young to control her magic and it was the middle of the night. Everyone was sleeping when the fire started. My entire family was killed."

"I'm so sorry." I touched his arm, making him stop in the forest. "But you didn't mean for anything like that to happen. You were a child."

"No, if I had been doing my duty instead of goofing off, they'd still be alive."

"You don't know that. If you had been there, you could've died too."

"What about you?" He lifted his chin. "You and your mom all this time? And why did she not teach you about your magic and how to use it?"

So it was that obvious? "My dad died five years ago, when I turned eleven. I thought it was from cancer."

"And that was not the case?" He gave me a sympathetic look.

"No." I shook my head, tears clogging my throat. What a fool I'd been thinking I could do magic without instruction and learning. The darkness lied. "H-he died protecting me. Never knew until Reed came to my house to bring me here."

"We have both suffered loss." He bowed his head to me.

"Yeah. We have." I gave him a smile.

"Now, we must finish our list, or we'll lose the scavenger hunt."

"Okay." I let out a breath. "It's basket on high, so a vine or something that grows up high, maybe in a tree."

Near us, an oak soared to the sky and I spotted green leaves with white berries. "Mistletoe?"

"Exactly."

"Great. How are we going to get that?" I gazed up at the tall tree.

"I'll boost you up." He clasped his hands in front of him.

"You sure about this?" I hesitated.

"You're not that heavy."

"How do you know how much I even weigh?"

"I doubt you are heavier than you look." He motioned with his hands and I reluctantly approached him.

"I'm blaming you if I break something." I put my foot into his hands.

In one swift movement, he stood lifting me up high. I scrambled for a nearby tree branch. My legs dangled underneath me.

"Don't you dare look up my skirt." I grunted, trying to get my purchase and partially flirting with him to see if I could get a rise out of him. He was so resigned and hard to read.

"Concentrate on not breaking your neck."

Finally, I got a better grasp and hefted myself up. I glanced down at him, there was a faint pink on his cheeks…so my comment earlier had embarrassed him. If I wasn't stuck up in the tree, I'd want to hug him for being so cute. The branch trembled underneath me. If I fell, I was so making Kento pay. I reached as far as I could for the next branch. It was thicker and should be able to support me better.

The limb beneath me started to crack.

"Keep moving."

"Tell me something I don't know." I pushed harder, stretching up to the other branch. The footing beneath me splinted. A yelp strangled in my throat. Flakes of oak and leaves cartwheeled to the ground. My nails dug into the bark of the branch above me, but I got one hand up and over.

I swung myself up, my uniform skirt snagging on the bark. My arms shook and I trembled with the effort of hauling myself up. I didn't even want to think about how I was going to get down.

The holly lay above me, still looked wicked far away.

"Hurry up, everyone's almost done gathering the ingredients," Kento called up to me.

He sounded like failing this assignment was the worst thing that could happen. It wasn't even his class! I ignored him, testing out the branch above me. This one snapped off in my hand and I wobbled, nearly tumbling.

Well, screw that. Now I had no leverage to reach the next branch and the mistletoe easily. I glared up at the plant, wishing the thing grew on the ground. The wind blew my hair in my face and sent a vine of mistletoe lower. Maybe I could reach it.

I stood on my tiptoes, straining while I held onto the tree's truck with one hand. But the vine was too far away, dangling above the end of the branch I was on.

Slowly, I inched out, stretching my hand as far as I dared, my fingertips almost brushing the spiny green leaves. Just a little further. The limb under my feet swayed with my weight and I bit my lip, creeping another fraction of an inch. My fingers flicked the plant and it swished away from me.

Crap!

I leaned forward. The plant swung back my way and I yanked on the vine. But my feet slipped.

I flailed, grasping at leaves and twigs to stop my fall. My body crashed into Kento and the air whooshed out of his lungs, but he held me, keeping my head from smacking in the ground.

"Sorry," I breathed out. My knee in his stomach and we were a tangle of arms and legs. Heat crept up my neck at our closeness. At our bodies touching and my skirt riding up. I pushed back when he locked his arms around me and I froze, mesmerized by his dark eyes and the expression of joy on his face. His breath fanned against my cheek and I nearly swooned from the intensity.

"That was the most amazing stunt I've ever seen. Too bad you didn't get any mistletoe."

"What are you talking about?" I opened my palm showing him the cluster of leaves I'd snagged, pride filling me.

His dark eyes lit up and I was suddenly aware of him

holding me. Of our bodies pressed close together. Of the way he was looking at me like he was debating kissing me.

"Kento—" I couldn't finish the words. Wanting him to kiss me, to feel his lips on me and know that he was as attracted to me as I was to him. How he was like a majestic mountain in my life. Steady, strong, and never changing. How I wanted to see him smile again—hell, I wanted to hear him laugh out loud and let loose with me.

His eyes took in my face, the intensity between us surged. I knew he wanted to kiss me. I could feel it with every fiber of my being. So why didn't he? I licked my lips and his gaze shifted to my mouth, my heart thumped.

"We cannot do this." He didn't look away.

His stare heating me all the way through. "Do what?" I breathed out.

"Zoey." He said my name like a prayer that had me leaning down, almost touching my lips to him.

"Ten minutes left," Mrs. Powell's voice rang out.

Embarrassed, I scrambled off Kento and stood, feeling a bit light-headed from our near kiss, while he slowly rose. "Okay. Tell me what's next and we'll gather as much as we can. Though if there's any more in a tree, it's your turn to risk your life."

"You were safe the whole time." He waved a hand and the branches that had fallen floated in the air.

"Jerk!" I pushed against his shoulder, teasingly. "You

could've lifted me up there. Or brought down the whole plant."

"And you wouldn't have the satisfaction of doing it yourself."

He was right, but he was still a jerk. "Fine. What's next?"

"Eye of newt is mustard seed — but the yellow ones, not the black."

"Do I even want to know why the colors matter?"

"Yellow is for positive things like birth, black for death." He pulled a torn leaf from my hair. "Tongue of dog is Gypsyflower. Adder's fork is Least Adder's tongue—a type of small fern. Wolf's Milk is Euphorbia and Dragon's blood is Calamus."

"All right." I rolled my shoulders back. "Even though we're hunting for plants and not animals, we are running out of time." Really didn't want to totally bomb my first class on my first official day.

Chapter 16

With one minute to spare, Kento and I raced back into class, my shoes squeaking across the linoleum.

Mrs. Powell cleared her throat. "I'm glad everyone was able to gather their ingredients. Now, what potion will be made from them?"

A few students raised their hand while I laid out the items we'd found across the tabletop.

"Zoey?" Mrs. Powell asked. "Any guesses?"

My whole face heated. I had no idea about any of it. "Is this something someone will drink?" Wasn't mistletoe or holly poisonous?

"So what do you think we'd be making?" Her voice light as she sat on the edge of her desk.

"A hexing potion?"

One of the girls in front of me snorted.

"Jezmaine, do you have the answer?" Mrs. Powell flicked a glance at her.

"Most of the items have a protective quality. So it has to be a banishing one or an increased potency of an existing spell."

"Very good. Both are correct."

The girl gave me a smug look. When Kento glanced up, she schooled her features. Let her think what she wanted, I bet she didn't climb a tree to get the mistletoe. Without their magic, many of these kids wouldn't last a week in my old school.

"Pull out your cauldrons and we start making the potion." Mrs. Powell walked between the tables, noting the students' gathered ingredients.

The cauldrons were in the cabinets under the tables and I hefted one out. It was black cast-iron and heavy. Mom had one in the attic I found once. Covered in cobwebs and stuffed in a corner. I asked her about it once and she blew off my question. When I pestered her, she said it had been a gift from my Aunt Ashlyn when they were girls, but that my mom had no talent for it. I had asked if she would teach me, but she said potions had to be taught by a good master or they'd all end up horrible likes hers did and she wasn't going to do that to me.

"Put your items into your cauldron," Mrs. Powell instructed, bringing me back to the present, "light the burner underneath it, then recite the incantation to make the potion."

She made it sound so easy. I scooped up our stuff from the table and dumped it into the cauldron. Then I took my potions book from my backpack, flipping through it for the right spell. When I glanced up, I noticed more than half the students were still carefully putting their plants and herbs into the pots.

Damn. Did I do something wrong again? From the corner of

my eye, I caught Kento watching me. "What?"

"Nothing." He fiddled with a small holly twig.

"Hey, thanks for being here—even though it's not your class." It was nice having someone I knew would talk to me and not treat me like a leaper. Even if it was because Olsen wanted one of them with me at all times.

"Just interested in how this is going to turn out."

"It'll be just fine," I said, though now I had serious doubts. Why did I keep screwing everything up? It was like I was jinxed. Except when I had embraced the darker magic to fight the Wendigos. I pushed the thought aside, blinking hard. I wasn't evil. I could do good things with my magic—I just needed more practice—I hoped.

"If it blows, duck behind me," Kento gave me a serious look, "I can shield you and the rest of the class from the blast."

"Thanks." I tucked my hair behind my ears and bent over the textbook. "Stir deosil three times, then widdershins once and repeat until mixture turns a bright green." I frowned. "What the heck does that mean?"

"Desoil is sunwise."

"Huh?"

"Sunward."

"How do I know what direction sunward is? Like up and down?" I moved the spoon in the cauldron.

"No." He grasped my hand to stop me, sweat beading on his

forehead. "Clockwise. Desoil is clockwise."

For a moment, I could only think about the feel of his hand over mine. I cleared my throat. "So widdershins is counterclockwise."

"Yes." As if realizing he hadn't moved his hand, he jerked it away quickly and I found I missed his touch.

I let out a huff. "Then why didn't they just say that or have a footnote or something?"

His mouth twitched up on one side and I noticed a dimple and a sparkle in his eyes. "We should ask the printers to update the books for those who might not know. It would've stopped me from having a gusher of octopus ink during my freshman year that I still don't think Mr. Bonds has recovered from."

I giggled and his smile widened. Soon I'd have him smiling all the time and laughing. He deserved to be happy. A thought that I could help him made me feel all warm and fuzzy inside.

"Remember to stir correctly." Mrs. Powell redirected one of the boys at the next table.

Reluctantly, I went back to stirring. Three times clockwise, once counterclockwise and repeat. When my brew started to bubble, I inched back.

"Is that a good sign or not?"

Kento frowned, staring into the cauldron, then a huge bubble popped into his face.

"Oh my god!" I yanked off my uniform blazer, wiping at his

face that was now covered with pink, sticky goo.

A rumble sounded from his chest and for a moment, I worried that he couldn't breathe.

"I'm so sorry, Kento. I-I didn't mean—" All of this carefulness and trying to do the right thing and I'd messed it up. "Wait. Are you laughing?"

He doubled over, tears pouring from his eyes, while pink taffy-like substance clung to his dark hair and over parts of his face. "It's laughing gum…I can't help it."

I glowered at the cauldron. Students around us were pointing and staring. A few looked so shocked that Kento was having this reaction like I'd ripped out his heart or something.

"Zoey." Mrs. Powell straightened her glasses. "Take Kento to the infirmary to remove the spell from him, then report to your next class."

I nodded, my face burning. I led Kento down the hallway to Nurse Jenkins. The bell to go to class rang.

"How long will this take?" I asked her as she used gloves and tweezers to pull out some of the pink goo from his face. If he was going to be awhile, I'd need a replacement chaperone for my next classes. Part of me liked the idea and the other part thought it was silly. I could take care of myself. *When I embraced the dark side of magic.* No, I couldn't think like that. Had to learn how to control my natural abilities and not depend on nefarious means.

His laughter filled the room. As nice as it was to hear, I wish it hadn't been from me doing the potion wrong.

"Give me about two hours. Then he'll be good as new." Jenkins removed another glob from his cheek.

At least he wasn't seriously injured. Except he was to be my chaperone until after lunch. I took out my cellphone from my pocket, fixing to send Jasper and Reed a message that I was going to Magic History without Kento. My fingers paused halfway through my text.

Why should I call my babysitters? I wasn't going to embrace the dark side of magic and become evil in one morning. And I knew the truth of them *protecting me* it was to keep an eye on me. I tucked my cell back into my pocket.

"Great. I'll come back by at lunch to check on him."

"Zoey," Kento laughed. "Wait…You… can't go… alone."

I flashed him a smile. "Don't worry. Everything will be fine. It's only history next, not like I can flub that up."

Before he could argue any more or Nurse Jenkins figure out that I needed constant observation, I squeezed out her door. The hallways stood empty with everyone already in their classes. Overhead, the tardy bell shrilled, and I cringed. I hated being late.

I ran around the corner when someone slammed into my back. My books and backpack scattered across the floor.

"Hey, watch—" My throat closed up as the dark figure cloaked in a hooded cape grasped me by the hair and lifted me, pressing my back to a row of lockers.

"You're a dark mage, like us," the raspy voice whispered.

"Is this a joke? Cause it's not funny." Leave it up to some bullies to do this then if I said yes, they'd run to Olsen and get me kicked out. *No way.*

The guy hauled me back my throat and slammed me against the lockers. My head rang with pain and I winced. He did it again until I had to blink to clear my vision.

"You will become one of us."

"Never." I struggled against the invisible hand on my throat and trying to get free. But I was pinned.

I opened my palm, sending out a spell that pinched my skin before hitting him. Instead of affecting him at all, it was like I hadn't done anything. But his cloak glimmered all over like it had somehow absorbed the magic. How was that possible?

"Your pathetic goody spells won't work against me." His hood still covered his face and I couldn't make out any features. "Embrace your true power."

Was he kidding? I'd seen what absolute power did. It was a one-way ticket to hatred and hurting others. The back of my mind teased that I could end this if I did what he said. If I let go of my restraints and shoved his body through the window behind him. That I could take his magic for myself, but keep it this time. I wouldn't have to return it. I could bury the body and hide the evidence. No one would know...

I shook my head, squeezing my eyes shut. "No."

"Then die."

Chapter 17

The invisible grip on my throat constricted harder, cutting off my air. I couldn't breathe. Spots danced before my eyes as I tried in vain to kick and punch the dark mage holding me. But each time I swung or thought I made contact, my fist or foot went right through his black cloak. It was like I was fighting the wind.

Spell after spell I heaved at him. Even the one I'd done on the bully, Darren, failed. My magic pricked across my palms like shards of ice, it rolled off me into the mage and he only squeezed harder.

I couldn't die like this. Not without seeing my mom one last time. Not without being able to hear Kento laugh again for real or kiss him. And I wanted to learn more about him and Jasper and Reed. I wanted them to admire me, not worry about me and fear what I would do. I wanted to do the right thing.

The first time I met Reed popped into my head and the hole in the classroom I'd caused. My hands buzzed a fraction. *Come on, come on!* Blackness spiraled my vision down to a pinprick. With all my strength and willpower I could gather, I forced my magic back. My palms itched and finally a spark shot out from them, slamming into the mage. He flew through the air into a pillar beside the window. Plaster crumbled around him.

I sank to the floor, gasping for breath, each inhale felt like razor blades to my throat.

"Nowhere is safe from your destiny, Zoey." The mage started to disappear before my eyes. "We will have you or your magic."

And just like that, he was gone. I choked, coughing as I tried to make sense of what just happened.

"Zoey?" Reed dashed down the hallway toward me. The fluorescent lights making his silver spiked hair gleam or maybe that was an aftereffect from me nearly dying. His gaze took me in, then my scattered books, and the hole in the pillar. "What happened?"

"I-I was attacked." I tucked my knees to my chest, wrapping my arms around them and rocked. *God, I almost died.* My whole body started trembling and I couldn't stop the shivers.

"By who? And why the hell didn't you tell me or Jasper that Kento was out of commission?"

"It just happened—there wasn't time to—" But there had been, and I'd chosen not to text or call them, because I thought I could handle everything on my own and go to one simple class like a normal, magical student. I chuckled at the irony and closed my eyes to keep the tears from falling. Here, I'd thought I was getting better. That I'd done the potion spell without a huge catastrophe only to have this happen now.

"Hey." Reed sank down beside me and put his arm around me, drawing me to his side. "Tell me what happened."

I scrubbed a hand down my face and opened my eyes. "A dark mage...he attacked me...wanted me to join them."

Beside me, Reed tensed but he didn't pull away or say anything.

"He was powerful, Reed. All my spells bounced off him— no, he like absorbed them—nothing worked."

"Is that what caused the hole over there?" he asked, pointing his chin at the pillar.

"A last-ditch effort. I remembered the time we met, and you dragged me into the classroom."

"Memories and emotions tied into magic can be very powerful. Then what happened? Did he run away, maybe we can catch him."

"No." I shook my head. "H-he disappeared. Right into thin air. How is that possible?"

"Dark magic gives abilities to those who practice it. But it comes at a cost. His soul and heart will have a void that only killing and taking magic from others can fill, temporarily."

I leaned back so I could see his face and try and read his expression. "So it's like being a vampire but instead of craving and needing blood, they need power?"

"Exactly." His face was a mask, but I knew he was thinking about what I'd said.

The mage's words replayed in my mind. If he was right, then this wouldn't be the last attack. "Reed, the mage said there were others always watching and nowhere was safe."

"We need to go to Olsen." His lips pressed into a thin line.

"Wait." I stifled a cough. "How do we know we can trust her?" *Or anyone?*

"We have to let Kento and Jasper know, at least, since we're the ones assigned to protect you." He stood and offered his hand. "We've known her a long time, but you're right—until we know for certain—we need to keep the group small. If you had told me a month ago that a student here was a dark mage and would have attacked you, I'd have thought you were mad. One of us is to be with you at all times. The other two can run reconnaissance and see if we can find out if Olsen is trustworthy or not."

"You sound like a spy," I teased.

"Sorry. I used to devour thrillers and spy novels as a kid." He shrugged a shoulder. "Guess some of it rubbed off. Wish I could know how to tell if someone is lying or not."

"You could give her a truth serum—I mean potion." I was still getting used to this magical world.

"Not a bad idea, but that one takes weeks to develop. In the meantime, we'll keep our ears and eyes open." He stared down at me. "And no more running off alone or I'll chain you to us."

Having a bodyguard now didn't seem like such a bad idea as it had before. *But the questions remain, why are the dark mages after me? Why now? Had they followed me here from home? Is my mom okay?*

While Reed talked to Jasper on the phone, I pulled out my cell. My mom hadn't texted me back and a seed of doubt burrows into me. She was probably just busy turning my room into a craft room. My whole life she'd jump from one to another. First it was cross-stitch, then painting, then crocheting.

I dialed her phone, but her voicemail came on. I tried to keep the concern and worry from leaking into my tone. "Hey, Mom, it's me. I've passed the first test and Headmistress Olsen has allowed me to take classes." I bit my lip, hating lying to her, though the truth would just worry her. "Things are great here. I've met some new friends and learning so much. I-I miss you. Call me when you can."

For a long time, I stared at my phone. Willing her to phone me right back. I wanted her to be proud of me and not look at me the way most of the students here did. At my old school, I was either invisible or a freak. Here, I was a novice that couldn't do anything right or a cold-blooded murderer. Kinda wish I could go back to being just Zoey.

Chapter 18

"I've brought Jasper up to speed and he's going to check on Kento." Reed's mouth twitched with humor. "Did you really get him laughing?"

"Not on purpose. The potion I was making turned into some type of pink goo. When it erupted in his face, he started laughing and couldn't stop." I had a feeling that none of the guys were going to let me live this down, because Kento was always serious and reserved.

"I'll have to stop at the infirmary after I drop you off, because I've known Kento since he started coming to the school when he was fourteen and I've never seen him even crack a big smile." He chuckled, shaking his head. "And I'm going to take a dozen pictures of him for blackmail later."

"Am I going to have to worry about payback from him? I mean will he take this out on me for doing this?"

"You'll have to take that up with Kento," Reed said matter-of-factly, but gave me a sidelong glance.

My stomach clenched. What would Kento do to me for hexing him?

Reed and I turned the corner. "In the meantime, what class

are you supposed to be in now?"

"I can't go to class now…" My throat ached from where I'd been choked. "There are dark mages around."

"Exactly, which is why we need to continue normalcy, schoolwork to get your mind off worrying." Reed tapped his temple. "They'll strike again, but this time we'll be expecting them. So what class?"

"Ugh, Magical History." Not that I wanted to do anything except crawl into bed and hide under the covers like I used to as a child when I couldn't sleep and thought there was a monster under my bed. But what else could I do? Pretend to be as normal as possible until those in charge found a way to help me? What else could I do except attend classes and try to figure out all this magic stuff so I could protect myself without fear.

"I'll walk with you to your class since all the hallways are empty. What do you have after History?" he asked.

Grabbing my backpack, I pulled out my schedule. "Tarot then lunch."

Reed nodded. "Jasper will meet us at lunch and take you to your other classes for the day. By then, Kento should be cured of the laughing hex you put on him."

"It was an accident." I cringed and stuffed my schedule back into my backpack. Fear hit me again about what Kento would do to repay me. Spiders in my locker? Shave my eyebrows? Or glue all my books closed?

"Let's go. You've got about forty minutes left of History," he said in an upbeat voice.

"Hey, why don't we switch? You sound excited about listening to a history lecture." I liked active classes, where participation and doing what was expected, not passively sitting listening to someone drone on an on while trying to stay awake and take notes.

"Are you kidding? How could you miss history?" He raked a hand through this silver hair. "I love it. Magical or Mundane. It all fascinates me."

"You are so weird," I said with a smile. "But in a good way."

He stood and held out his hand to help me up. When my palm touched his and he laced his fingers with mine, warmth spread through my body. But all too soon, he broke off our contact. Did he feel the connection like I did? Or was it all business— protect the new kid from the dark monsters—collect the reward, move on. The memory of Olsen congratulating him on finding me flashed through my mind. What if he just needed to keep me safe so he could graduate with honors? It shouldn't bother me, but it did. I felt like I was developing a crush on him and Jasper and Kento, but they had another agenda that didn't include me in their future. Or maybe I was just being paranoid.

We walked to history which was a lecture hall with chairs and tiny desks that only had room to lay a notebook and pen on top off. I looked back to wave at Reed, but he was already gone. The fact he hadn't waited around to make sure I was settled stung a little bit.

"During the burning times, our kind went underground," the teacher, a man with thick glasses and thinning hair spoke from the front of the room, oblivious to our tardiness as he had his back to the class. His hand drew out a rune on the board. "This was the symbol used to identify a coven. Witches were expected to have no more than thirteen in a group. Anyone care to guess why?"

He faced the audience and searched the few hands that were raised.

"Ah, Simon, I know you remember this from last year. Would you care to share with the class the answer?"

Simon's face colored red, but he nodded. "The number was thirteen, to keep the coven small, in case they were discovered."

"Exactly." The teacher went back to writing on the board. This time drawing an inverted rune with a slash through it. "And what was expected if one of the coven members were caught by the humans?"

"To never betray another member," Simon said.

"And to do so?" The teacher turned back to the class, this time pointing to Megan in the front row.

"It was the worst betrayal a witch could do to another. They were labeled as Oath Breakers as they broke their sacred oaths never to reveal another member of the coven." She looked over her shoulder at me, then whipped her head back around.

Had she felt the dark mage attacking me earlier? Did she even care?

"There is another form of betrayal, does anyone know that one?"

Megan lifted her hand again but spoke before the teacher could acknowledge her. "Yes, anyone who practices magic to intentionally harm another or to gain personal power is considered dark magic. One who practices the dark magical arts."

"Yes. With our society completely ostracized from the humans, we grew in power and some of us in pride. Many tried dark magic to gain abilities and force their will over others." The teacher paced in front of the class. "They were captured and executed. Evil breeds contentment and heinous crimes in the name of selfishness. These individuals didn't care about others or improving the magical community, only their own gain."

If the dark mages were executed, how come they were still around? I glanced at the students in the class. Some doodled in their notebooks, others sent text messages when the teacher wasn't looking their way, others yawned or whispered to their neighbor. Any one of them could have been the one who attacked me.

Was I safe here—even with Jasper, Kento, and Reed? Could they protect me and the other students if a dozen dark mages came after us? If another attack hit the school?

I didn't think I could embrace the dark power as I had

before without it digging its claws deeper into my soul. How long before I wasn't able to fight back? Before I became evil and no longer cared who I hurt?

Chapter 19

I unhooked my backpack off my chair and strolled to the Tarot class when I didn't find Reed or Jasper waiting for me outside history. Fear trickled down my throat, but I pushed aside the feeling. They didn't need to escort me everywhere. I was totally capable of walking to class with the rest of the students. Except, I did miss their company. What if they figured I wasn't worth the trouble? Can't say that I blamed them—I wouldn't want to hang out with anyone dark mages had targeted if I could help it.

Stop! God, I needed to get a grip on my emotions. Everything was fine. I needed to get my mind off worrying like Reed said and focus on school.

I'd never been able to practice or learn the divination technique. The more I was here, the more I realized Mom had almost been afraid of magic or to use it. I knew she'd said my Aunt Ashlyn had mental issues and magic had destroyed her, but I took it for granted that my mom was a witch and had taught me enough not to injure myself. Now I understood that she'd taught me as little as possible.

I didn't blame her. Seeing magic twist someone close had to be a difficult thing to witness. Especially when there was nothing to do to help.

God, I missed Mom. I snuck a glance at my phone. No return calls or messages. My gut clenched. *Why hasn't Mom responded to me? Is something wrong?*

I followed the other students piling into the room. This class was arranged with small tables and a chair on each end.

Megan sat at an empty table, cards stacked in front of her.

At the front of the room sat a thin-looking man who wore a bright purple robe and his dark hair was combed to the side. His nose took up half his face, but his eyes were kind.

Quickly, I glanced around the classroom for another empty seat, but the only one was in front of Megan. She avoided my gaze. I had no choice. It was either stand and look more awkward than I already was, or join her.

I approached her table and gestured to the chair. "May I?"

"Whatever." She pushed back from the table, picking at her nails rather than glance up at me.

I sat down, crossing my legs under the table. The cards between us were bigger than I expected them to be. I had thought tarot cards were the size of regular playing cards, but these were about the size of my hand from wrist to fingertips. They were face down and had a black background with golden vines and silver flowers decorated on them.

"Afternoon, class. I'm Mr. Halon. Welcome our new student, Zoey and now we have an even number of tarot readers and querents. We've moved from one-card draws to two. Today, we'll do a three-card draw. First card will be the querent's past, second card the present, and the third will be the future."

I raised my hand.

"Yes, Miss Dane?"

"Sorry, what's a querent?"

Megan snorted and two more students snickered under their breath.

"Excellent question for newcomers." The teacher smoothed a hand down the collar of his purple robe. "The querent is the person drawing the cards—the person seeking the answer in the tarot."

My face burned that I didn't know a simple answer like that. Why hadn't my mom at least taught me the basics?

"Right. Each of you has a partner. One of you pick three cards and the other will try to interpret." Mr. Halon walked around the tables. "Of course, the past and possibly the present will be able to tell you if your reading is accurate. The future, well, that is never set in stone. Decisions and circumstances can change. So whatever you draw as the third card is only one possibility of your future. Now take turns. The first person draws three cards and your partner interprets. Then switch roles and repeat."

"You can go first." I motioned to Megan. Partially because I wasn't even sure how to do this.

"I'll draw first if that's what you mean." She straightened.

I bit back a comment when I saw the white scar lines running down one cheek and onto the side of her neck, knowing that it was my fault that she was scared. "Great."

She shuffled the cards, then laid three cards face down. I stared at them. Was I supposed to guess what she'd drawn? I stole a glance at the other tables. Kids bent over the table, but they'd turned the first card over and were talking in hushed whispers.

Okay. I flipped the first card over. A woman with a crown reclined on a throne. Her white dress was tied with a golden belt that dangled onto a floor with two black cats playing with the end. Underneath the card read, The Empress.

"It's beautiful." All of the colors and detail of the drawing were breathtaking.

"Wait—you've never seen tarot cards before?" Megan asked, incredulously.

"No." I traced a finger along the edge. "Mom didn't embrace her magical side. We never had these in our house, and she forbade me to go into any magic stores—even the human ones."

"Well, I'm sure you'll catch on quick." Megan narrowed her eyes like she didn't believe me, her words cutting and snide. "You seem to not have any problems with dark sorcery."

I forced aside my anger. "Right. Empress. So I guess you thought you were a queen? Or your mother was?"

"The cards aren't literal like that…at least not all the time."

She bristled. "This is saying that I had a confident mother who raised me to be like her."

I turned over the second card. A hanged man, but he was hanging by his foot. "This means that you are in limbo or a kind of holding pattern."

"It means I need to let go of something. A sacrifice." There was a pinch to the corners of her eyes.

The final card showed a man staring up at the clouds, dressed in robes like a nobleman but about to walk off a cliff. "Fool card." I stared at it, trying to decipher its meaning because I knew it wasn't a message of *watch where you're going* like it depicted. "Does it mean anything different because it's upside down?"

"Yes, a reversal." She crossed her arms and leaned back. "It means the opposite, usually, of what the card means facing the correct way."

"Okay. Reversed, it almost looks like he's already fallen off the cliff. So a warning?"

She shrugged a shoulder.

"Uncertainty or—"

"Very good, Zoey," Mr. Halon said behind me. "Confusion and a lack of self-confidence. Exactly the opposite of Megan's past card, the Empress. Now put all three together."

I squirmed in my seat. "So she moved from being confident in the past to a place of needing to sacrifice something." Pride popped into my mind, but I didn't say it. Megan already hated me. I didn't need to add fuel to that fire. "And if she doesn't, she'll become like the upside-down fool, losing her assurance."

"Exactly." He beamed. "Now. You shuffle the deck and draw out three cards and let Megan interpret them."

When he moved to the next table, I did as he asked, adding back the three read cards and re-shuffling. Suddenly the deck felt hot in my hands, I frowned, worried that my magic was going to incinerate them.

"What's wrong?" Megan asked in a small, panicked voice.

"The cards...they feel hot...like they're going to catch fire."

"That means to stop shuffling." She shook her head. "Wow, you really don't know much about magic, do you?"

I cleared my throat and set down the cards. Then I laid out the top three as she had done.

The first card she turned over showed a devil holding the chains of a man and a woman.

"What does that mean?" It couldn't be good.

"Um..." She frowned. "In your past, there was a pact of some kind. Instant gratification, slave to desires, chained to negative forces."

"That doesn't make any sense."

"Maybe the other cards will clarify it." She turned over the second card. This one was named The Magician and showed a guy with a wand holding it high overhead. A table was before him with a pentacle, sword, rod and cup.

"Those are the four elements," I said, and she nodded.

"The Magician says that you have all of the tools you need inside you to ensure that success is manifested. It's about making something happen and is tied to your instinct and intuition."

"Or it could just mean I'm at a Magical Academy to learn how to use my talents and abilities."

Briefly, she cracked a smile at that. "Aren't we all?"

When she turned over the third card, she paled. It was of a person lying in bed with ten swords in their back.

"Is that the death card?" I shivered.

"No, but it's kinda worse."

"How can it be worse than death? The guy is stabbed ten times, looks pretty dead to me." I swallowed the lump suddenly in my throat.

"No, the death card can be about change. It's rarely about a physical, real death."

"And this one?" My voice came out in a hoarse shriek.

"Deep wounds, obviously." She glanced up at me. "It also means painful endings, loss, crisis and betrayal. I-I don't see how these three ties in together. Why don't you shuffle again?"

With shaking hands, I did as she asked, laying out three cards. When she turned them over, one at a time, it was the same ones. There wasn't any denying it. My future held sorrow and death. I had to get to my mom before it was too late.

Chapter 20

"Tarot isn't for everyone," Megan said, and I wondered how pale I looked for her to be nice to me.

"But it's accurate. I mean I drew the exact same cards...twice."

The teacher came over to our table. "What's wrong?"

"It's the same cards." I blinked back tears. "Look at my future card."

"Remember," he crossed his arms behind his back. "It's not set in stone. The future is ever-changing, flexible."

I tried to let his words comfort me, but they didn't. He turned to another table to help them with their interpretation of the cards.

How was it that I drew all three cards again? Wasn't that a sign that this was a big deal? A warning?

Mom. I grabbed my backpack and dug through it for my cell.

I checked my messages. Nothing. No calls, no text, nothing. Panic squeezed my chest. She would've contacted me. Made sure I made it to school safely. Called and would want the latest gossip and how I was setting in and about my classes. I had to go see her.

At the thought of telling the guys, I could just picture Reed's reaction, he'd tell me that I was safer here at school. But was I really?

I pushed back, standing and slinging my backpack over my shoulder.

"Where are you going?" Mr. Halon asked.

"I've got to go, I can't stay here."

"If she wants to go, let her," Megan smirked.

I didn't care that she was only on my side right now to get rid of me. There was no way I could stay here if my mom was in trouble.

When I dashed out of the classroom and ran toward the exit, I crashed right into Reed. *Fuck!*

"Hey, where are you going?"

I hiccupped a cry. "The tarot cards say Mom is or will be in danger soon if I do nothing."

"You don't know that." The muscle in his jaw twitched.

"Yes, I do. I drew the same exact cards twice in a row. It's my mom, now get out of my way." I pushed past him, but he held onto my arm.

"Let us send an inquiry. Find out what's going. We can even bring her here for a brief visit. Would that make you feel better?"

I looked away. As soon as he was gone, I'd go to Headmistress Olsen. Get a pass to go home and see what she said. Truth was, everything in me said to go now. This instant. I doubted that Olsen would agree. She'd probably say to wait, and they would look into the matter just like Reed, which meant I would need to sneak out when he and the other guys weren't around.

After the bell rang to go to lunch, I ducked into the girl's bathroom. The one place Reed couldn't follow me. A girl in a hoody smoked a cigarette in the corner.

"Oh, it's you. I thought you were a teacher." She took a puff.

I needed a way to get past Reed and the Headmistress too at least for a few minutes so I could get supplies for leaving. "Um…hey, I like that sweater. Would you be willing to sell it to me?"

She looked down at herself. "Sure. How much you got?"

"Twenty?"

"Paid twice that for it." She took a long drag on her cigarettes.

"Fine. Fifty and I can give it back to you later. I just need to borrow it."

"Whatever, give me the money first."

I dug in my wallet and handed her out tens and a couple of five-dollar bills to equal the agreed upon amount. Then she laid her cigarette on the edge of the sink, took off her jacket, and handed it back to me.

"I want it cleaned too, before you give it back."

"Already planned on it." I smiled at her, then yanked the

hoody over me, keeping the hood on and shoving my black hair inside. It reeked of smoke, but hey, at least if Reed had a good sense of smell, he'd never know it was me.

Before the next bell rang, I pushed open the bathroom door, holding my breath. I was sure Reed would figure out it was me. I kept my head down, and hunched my shoulders, rushing down the hallway. When no one ran after me or called my name, I relaxed some. It would only be a little bit of time before Reed realized I wasn't in the bathroom anymore and came looking for me.

My heart beat fast as I hurried.

I stopped off at my dorm. I needed to drop off my books and stuff my backpack with clothes and money for the trip back home. When I opened my door, a waft of something citrusy hit me. *What the hell?*

Everything seemed to be in order. My bed made from this morning. Nothing out of place. Uneasiness pressed into my gut though. I dumped out my books onto my nightstand, then quickly yanked open drawers and pushed a couple of underwear, jeans, and some T-shirts into my bag. I went into the small bathroom to grab my hairbrush when I saw it.

Written in black ink was the message, *We're coming for you.*

Shaking, I tried to wipe the message off the mirror, but it wouldn't come off. Tears stung the back of my eyes. I didn't have time for this. I had to get to my mom. This place wasn't any better at protecting me than my own home. I had to get out of here now.

I picked up my backpack and yanked open the door to find Reed standing there with his arms crossed over his chest.

"Holy fuck! You nearly gave me a heart attack," I said, placing a hand to my breastbone.

He lifted a hand, plucking at the material of the hoody. "Nice try."

Let him think what he wanted. I was going to be out of here before next period. "Can't blame a girl for trying."

"It's not safe out there, Zoey. You have to trust me."

I didn't want him to see the message on the mirror, so I closed my door behind me. "I-I know. I just hate waiting and not knowing what's going on."

"We'll figure it out," he said softly.

I nodded, walking briskly away. If he saw my face, he'd know something was wrong, I couldn't risk that. If he read the message than it would be even worse. He and the others would probably glue themselves to my side and even attend classes with me. I'd never get a chance like this again. I had to escape after lunch. The need to see my mom raging through me. "I'm starving. Let's go get some food."

At lunch, my legs bobbed under the table, my pizza slice

only half-eaten. Reed had taken off to collect his class assignments for the ones he missed this morning and Kento was still with the nurse from what Jasper had told me when he slid on the bench across from me.

"You gonna finish that?" Jasper asked, eyeballing my plate.

I pushed it forward, glancing at my cellphone.

"Expecting someone's text?" he asked and pushed half the pizza in his mouth.

How could he even breathe with that much food in his mouth? "Um…no."

"You have the guiltiest look on your face," he said between mouthfuls. "What's up?"

Maybe it would be good to have one of the guys on my side. Otherwise, how was I going to leave without one of them knowing? I couldn't wait for Reed to get whatever team together to go check on my mom, I needed to do it now. This place wasn't safe. The dark mages were here, and I had a feeling things were only going to get worse. If I could go back to Mom, we'd figure something out. After she heard what had happened here at the academy, she'd have to agree with me. We could leave the city and find somewhere safe. She could teach me about my magic more and how to control it. Had to see now that it was a necessity. Being on the run would buy us some time before the dark mages found us. Or we might avoid them altogether. It was a better shot than staying here and waiting for them to come to me. But Jasper was right, I had to have one of them on my side or they'd know within minutes, like Reed had, that I was gone.

"Okay, promise you won't tell anyone? Especially not Reed or Kento?"

"Is it a prank like what you did with Kento, priceless by the way." He winked. "Once I put a hair removal potion in their shampoo. It was a gradual thing. For a whole month, they thought they were going bald early. God, that was so fun."

"That's kind of mean, is it?"

"Oh, they got me back. Knocked me out and made a spell to remove every shred of hair on my entire body." He leaned forward, whispering, "Like everything...eyebrows, eyelashes. Shit, I didn't even have nose hairs for months."

I laughed despite my worry over my mom. "Well, this isn't a joke, per se. I-I just need to get out of the academy for a bit."

"Keep talking." He stared at me with curiosity and his response startled me.

"Just for the day to check on my mom." I pushed my phone toward him. "She hasn't contacted me since I got here and isn't responding to my calls or messages."

His fingers brushed over the phone, but he didn't glance down at him, his eyes staring at me. "A little hooky? Sounds like fun."

"Thank you." I reached across the table and I took my phone back. "Reed already knows about the trouble but doesn't understand my urgency. He wants me to wait. I can't, Jasper. This has been slowly eating me up from the inside for days and today I got a message that my future is going to be horrible if I don't go do this. Now."

"Whoa." He held up his hands. "What message?" Then he lowered his voice, leaning forward. "The dark mage didn't tell you this, did he? Cause I'd say that's bogus then, but we can still sneak out. I'm all for ditching the rules. We can check out the latest slasher movie in town."

I shook my head. "It was from a tarot card reading. I drew the exact same cards, in the same order, twice. I have to see my mom."

"All right." He picked up the last of the pizza. "Let's go."

"Wait, just like that?" I scrambled to stand, my backpack caught on the edge of the table.

"It's the best time." He took a huge bite of the pizza. "Isn't that what you were thinking?"

I nodded, my throat suddenly closing that he would be willing to do this with me and for me. "Let's go."

Chapter 21

"Can you take off that hoody? It's making you smell like a bad perfume factory bathed in smoke." Jasper pinched his nose and made a face.

"Sure." I took off the hoody and stuffed it into my locker. The girl I borrowed it from might get mad that I didn't get it cleaned or returned it to her, but she had gotten compensated enough. Not like I'd ever come back here or have to see her or anyone else from the academy again. My stomach clenched at the thought. God, I'd miss Jasper, Reed, and Kento. I'd gotten used to having them around.

Jasper took my elbow and led me down to the gymnasium, which was eerily quiet and empty. Must be no classes here right now. No wonder Jasper picked this place for us to come to and avoid being seen by anyone.

Once I got home, I'd figure out how to tell him I wasn't coming back. One problem at a time. Right now, my mom was more important than anything else, even hurting Jasper's feelings. Though the idea of what he'd think, sent a hot poker of dread into my heart. And Kento…he'd finally started to open up to me, sharing about his past and the loss of his family. Would he close up again with that reserved demeanor and never let anyone close to him again? The poker twisted. And Reed. He'd been the one to bring me here. To convince me that I could fight the Wedingos and not keep his and the other guys' powers. I'd let them all down.

I pushed those aside I followed Jasper to the gym, needing to focus on Mom. They'd understand, they had to. His humming the theme song to Mission Impossible brought a small smile to my face.

When we pushed inside the double doors, the scent of rubber basketballs and tennis shoes nearly knocked me over. "What are we doing in here? The parking lot is on the other side of the school."

"We're not taking a vehicle." Jasper jogged over to a closet.

"Why not? I'm not walking that far—I've enough for a bus pass for both of us."

"Oh, ye of little faith." He whispered some magic words at the lock and the door popped open. A few soccer balls tumbled out, but he kicked them aside. One sailing across the gym's floor and bounced into the bleachers.

"Nice shot," I joked.

"Been on the team since I was ten." He dug through the metal shelves of P.E. supplies, then pulled out a thick piece of chalk.

"What's that for?" I asked, backing up out of the closet.

"Normally for marking drills, but today it's our ticket out of here."

"If you say so. You going to draw a portal for us to step through?" This was a magical academy and I'd seen stranger things since I'd come here.

"Not exactly, but super close." He moved to behind the bleachers and drew out a circle around himself, before he closed it off, he waved me over. "Hurry up and get inside so I can close it."

I stepped next to him. Then he drew the chalk around, sealing us in. My guess was he drew it back here so when he returned, no one would notice him suddenly popping in.

"Okay," he breathed. "Imagine your home. The house. The tree in the front yard and flowerbed. Picture the windows and as much detail as you can."

"And if I mess this up?" I couldn't stop myself from asking.

"We might end up in someone else's yard at best." He brushed aside the sandy hair out of his eyes. "Or in limbo, in between worlds forever."

"Gez, no pressure."

"You can back out now." He placed his hands on my shoulders until I looked up at him. "But I've seen you handle much harder stuff than this."

"Like the match?" The words scraped my throat.

A shadow crossed his features, but he pushed it aside as quickly as it came. Though I knew what he was thinking...that I was going to somehow mess this up. That the only magical talent I had was for being a horrible jinx or skating too close to the dark side that I might eventually fall all the way over and become evil.

"You've done more than that since then. What have you got to lose?"

"Oh, I don't know, getting lost in a black hole?" I bit the inside of my cheek, fear escalating in my chest.

"We don't have time for that, right? This is the fastest, easiest way. It will buy us some time before Reed and Kento figure out we're gone. If we take regular transportation, they'd just zoom over and bring us back before we even get out of town. Is that what you want?"

I shook my head. "No. They'll be on high alert and I might never get a chance like this again."

"Exactly. Now, let's do this."

"Yes." I had to see Mom. I closed my eyes and imagined my home as I'd left it before I came here. Down to the crack along with the front window when I'd accidentally tossed a rock too hard, but it hadn't broken the glass.

"Tolle de nobis temporis et spatii, in quo non vis," Jasper whispered. "Take us between the world of here and now to where we wish to go."

There was a whooshing sound all around me. Then suddenly, it felt like all the air had been sucked out of my lungs and around us.

"Keep your focus, Zoey," Jasper yelled, but it sounded like

he stood miles away from me.

I was too frightened to open my eyes. To break my concentration if I saw us hurling through space. I gasped, trying to draw in air. My lungs convulsed. Spots danced before my eyes. I tightened my grip on Jasper's arms.

My eyes flew open, when we fell onto tall grass. The blades scratched against my bare legs and I pulled my school uniform down. I should've changed into jeans before doing this. Untangling my backpack from a shrub bush, I glanced around. This wasn't my home. It was an abandoned field that I used to come out to practice my magic.

"Where are we?" Jasper asked, scratching his head. "I thought I remember your house looking different."

"It's not my house, come on, it's just up the block and around the corner." I went to put on my backpack, but Jasper took it from me carrying it.

Mom would know my feelings the moment she saw us even though he didn't hold my hand or anything. She'd always been good at reading when people liked each other. Even to the point where others would get mad at her and tell her she was crazy. But sure enough, after a little time went past, her predictions would come true.

Of course, what would she think if she knew I was not only attracted to Jasper, but Kento and Reed as well? When I was with one of them then it seemed right to be with them. And when all three were around me, I felt different. Protected, yes in a sense, but also cherished. More than that. I couldn't quite put my finger on it. I felt connected and part of a whole.

We hiked up the path to the subdivision, my heart beating faster with each step. Soon I'd be able to see Mom. Hug her and smell her scent of lilacs and flour. She was always cooking stuff. I'd tell her everything that had happened and that we'd been wrong, the academy couldn't protect me. She and I needed to leave, like I'd first suggested when Reed had come to my house, and find a safe place just the two of us.

I pushed aside the unease feeling clawing its way up my spine. The message on the mirror and the tarot cards along with the dark mages attack on the school and on me.

"Which way?" Jasper asked at a fork in the road.

"Left then my street curves around. Fifth house on the left."

A breeze tugged at my skirt as we walked. At least it wasn't raining today. The autumn sun twinkled overhead against a turquoise sky.

Then we turned on my street and my pace increased. I dragged Jasper after me as I started to run. My heart beating frantically in my chest. But as we rounded the corner, something was off. The chimney and the sloped roof wasn't visible. We should see it by now.

I stumbled over a tree root running across the sidewalk that had broken through the cement. Jasper kept me from falling.

"Thanks," my voice came out hoarse and scratchy.

What is going on? I drew nearer to my house, the green grass and flowerbeds were crushed and black. I stopped short, my heart turning to ice.

It was gone. My entire home was burnt to the ground. Nothing remained but a huge black hole. Only a few scattered, broken bricks remained of the fireplace.

I sank to my knees, trembling. *Mom!* I couldn't move. I couldn't even think. This had to be a horrible dream. A nightmare that I would wake up from and be so relieved it wasn't real.

"Zoey—" Jasper knelt beside me.

"Wha—What happened?" I blinked back tears, my heart shredding. "What could have done this?"

"Magic." He frowned. "Very dark magic."

A sob escaped my mouth. "And my mom…where is she?"

"I-I don't know."

I stood, shaking all over. "Where is she, Jasper? Y-You did the spell wrong. We're in the wrong time or dimension or some shit."

"No, I did the spell perfectly. This is now. This is the reality."

I shook my head, shoving my hands into his chest. "No! You fix this. You redo it. This c-can't be what happened. Do the spell again."

"It won't change anything," he said quietly. "It's like your tarot cards, you can keep shuffling, keep re-drawing, but you'll get the same answer."

I refused to let him be right. He couldn't be. My mom couldn't be gone. She couldn't be ash like the rest of the house. I wouldn't allow it.

Clenching my fists, I swallowed down what felt like shards of glass in my throat and marched up the path to the blackened crater that had been my home.

"Where are you going?" Jasper called out as he ran to catch up to me.

"To find out who did this and fight the bastards."

Chapter 22

I stomped over the threshold into the blackened ground that used to be my home. Sorrow clung to me, but rage was slowly building underneath. I wanted to bring my mother back. I wanted to make those who did this pay. I wanted to have a future where I wasn't alone and had my family.

This left me with nothing. I had to make a choice between the evil that did this or the magical academy. Neither choice was perfect. First of all, because I hated the sorcerers who did this and I would fight until my last breath to stop them. And second, I didn't fit in with the witches and wizards at school. I was an outsider just as I was before. Third, I really didn't want to leave Jasper, Kento, or Reed.

But right now I had to end this. Had to avenge my mother's pointless death. How long ago had this happened? Two days? The day I left for the academy?

I knelt, digging my fingers through the blackened earth and ash, clenching my fist and letting the fragments of my past and present crumble. My magic zinged across my palms and up my arms. It felt like ants trying to get out of my skin, biting and nipping at me, but I held onto it.

"Zoey, God, what are you doing?" He panted, coming up beside me.

"What I should've done that first day Reed and you and Kento came to collect me."

"This place reeks of evil magic, don't you feel it?" He glanced around, his eyes wide.

All I felt was hollow, an emptiness that would never fade.

"Go back to the academy, Jasper." I stood. "What I'm about to attempt is dangerous and I don't even know if it will work." But I couldn't do nothing. I had to try, even if it killed me too in the process.

"Shit, whatever it is you're thinking of doing, don't. W-We can get a crew out here and find out who did this. Let our justice system deal with them." Sweat beaded his brow.

"Thank you for everything and for bringing me here, but I have to do this. I have to try."

"Please, just wait." Jasper's brow furrowed. "We can get Reed and Kento to help. We'll do whatever we can, but don't open your magic like this. You haven't learned how to control your emotions or your powers after this great loss."

"I've waited long enough and look at what these bastards did." I dug my nails into my palms, my blood mixing with the fragments of dirt in my hands. "They destroyed my home... what if they killed my mom?"

He glanced away and I marched around him to make him

face me.

"What?" My throat tightening with unshed tears and ragged emotions. "Tell me."

"There's a way we can tell." He let out a sigh. "But I'm worried how you'll take it if the news isn't good."

"Do it." My chin quivered, but I lifted my head to stop it. "I have to know if she's okay and they just took her or—" I couldn't finish the words.

"Hic revelare secreta," he said, picking up one of the blackened, crumbled bricks. The fragment shattered in his hand, then danced over his palm, making an outline of a woman.

"Mom," I cried out, hugging myself. But then the debris changed to a skull and my heart shattered, tears stinging my eyes.

"I'm sorry, Zoey," the pity in his voice was my undoing, but I backed from his outstretched arms.

"No, no, you're wrong." She couldn't be dead. I bit my lip, tasting blood and wrapping my arms around my middle. "T-The skull means something else. Like-Like it's a clue to who took her."

"Zoey." He stepped forward, his arms still out for me.

I let out a strangled cry as it felt like I was coming apart inside. That I'd never be the same and I knew I wouldn't. *Mom!* I trembled, falling to my knees. "I will kill whoever did this. I will hunt them down like the animals they are."

"I know, I know." He reached out to touch my shoulder when an arc of power hit his hand and he cursed, shaking his arm.

"This isn't the way, Zoey. You'll become just like the ones that did this."

"This is your first and last warning, Jasper, go back to the academy." I squeezed my eyes shut as my magic zinged up my back and crawled over my skull. "You can bring back whoever you wish, but I hope to be finished one way or another before then."

"I'm not leaving."

His words cut into my soul, but I had to continue. I had to do this. I opened my eyes and he sent a text on his phone which I guessed was to Kento and Reed. I shrugged. They wouldn't stop me. Not until I crushed whoever was responsible for all of this.

"With my blood and will, I summon the evil who burnt this house to the ground. And find out what happened to my mom." I opened my hands, letting the few drops of my blood and dirt to fall. My magic lashed out of me like a whip.

I sank to my knees, trembling from the use of power. Black lightning flashed across the sky. And then shadows and darkness filled the space. It was as though someone had turned off the sun.

Eyes blinked, staring at me. A sense of foreboding clamping down on my throat.

"Who are you to summon us?"

"Zoey Dane. It is my house and my mother whom you have hurt, and I will repay you in kind."

"Such brave talk, from one who doesn't even embrace her

true self."

I straightened. Whatever these things were, they didn't realize I would use whatever I had, whatever I could to make the pain and loss of my mother bearable. Right now it was eating a hole in my heart and I would do anything to ease the pain. And going out with a bunch of evilness was just icing on the cake.

"That's where you're wrong." I opened myself up to the power buried deep inside me. The one that coursed through my veins and echoed between each heartbeat.

"Zoey, no!" Jasper yelled. His magic striking down the dark mages close to me.

But they brushed off their robes like he'd done nothing. I knew regular, by-the-rules magic wouldn't work on them. It hadn't with the wraith or the Wendigos or the one who attacked me in the hallway.

I sent my power out. It ripped from me and launched into the dark mages. They fell to their knees, their screams filling my ears and I reveled in the joy of it. Of making them suffer. Did they show my mom mercy? Then I would show them none either.

They sent blow after blow of magic, it lashed across my flesh, drawing blood but I didn't care. Grief and adrenaline fueled me. They wouldn't be able to stop me unless they killed me, but I wouldn't give them the chance.

My magic surged into more of the mages and they too fell to their knees, gripping their throats and trying to get air into their lungs. I imagined their eyes bulging, their hearts stopping. I poured into them all my sorrow and loss.

The ground shook beneath me and I felt powerful again. Like I could do no wrong. I wasn't as strong as when I fought the Wendigos, as I didn't have the guys' borrowed magic, but what I did have was fueled with such hatred that I felt like I could tear the world apart.

"This won't change anything, Zoey. Stop before the darkness takes over you," Jasper wheezed out.

I stared at him, trying to decipher his words and why he was having a hard time talking. That's when I realized that my magic was attacking him just like the dark sorcerers.

No! I tried to haul my power back, but it was like a rabid dog that had gotten free from its leash. It bit into me and snarled and didn't heed my will.

"If you kill them," Jasper's face turned purple as he choked, trying to breathe. "You'll become like t-them."

I slammed my hands into the ground. "Stop!" My body shaking, trembling. The shadows around me closed in, hungry. Tearing at my clothes, my flesh, craving my blood and my magic. Feasting on my emotions.

"Stop, please," I cried, digging my fingers into the ash. Letting myself feel the agony of Mom's death. How I wasn't here to help her. How I'd let her down and she'd be so disappointed if she saw me now. How she was the only family I had after Dad had died. And he'd sacrificed his life to protect me from this. My mom must have as well.

The darkness wailed against me, choking my air off, suffocating my powers. I twisted, pushing out everything I had to stop the onslaught. But the rapids kept pulling me under. Depression sank in my middle, weighing me down. It didn't matter how powerful I was or thought I was, I was nothing but one small life against a riptide of evil.

Suddenly, a snap vibrated through my entire being. I fell on my stomach across the ground.

"Zoey!" someone shouted.

I blinked, trying to focus. Where were the mages? Everything around me was hazy.

"Jasper?" my voice sounded hoarse and weak.

Then Kento turned me over and pulled me into his arms. I looked over his shoulder to find Reed standing there with a mix of fury and worry etched on his face.

I pushed back, letting Kento help me stand, my whole body feeling like I had the flu or something.

"What the hell, Zoey," Reed spat out. "I told you to wait. Why would you pull a stunt like this?"

I sank against Kento's side. What I'd done wasn't enough, not by a long shot, but it was a start. It showed me that I needed the academy. Needed these three men in my life to help show me how to harness my power and not let it get out of control or overpower me.

"The enemy surrounded us out of nowhere," I said hoarsely, still reeling from my mom's death. "We had to do something and stop them."

"Us?" Kento frowned.

"Who else was here?" Reed asked with his face turning dark.

A cold sense of dread wrapped around me like a wet blanket. "J-Jasper." I spun out of Kento's grasp, searching the devastation for Jasper. He was nowhere. No sign that he'd even ever been here with me along with the three mages. Had I killed him like the mages had done to my mom?

"Oh god." I covered my mouth with a trembling hand as the realization shook me to my core. "He's gone."

I turned my gaze to Reed. "Please, tell me he's not dead. That he went back to the academy."

"His magic signature tells me that his heart stopped here." Reed pointed to the spot. "Then there's nothing but intense heat."

"D-Do the reveal spell that he did," I clung to Kento. "The one that told him what happened to my mom. We have to be sure."

But Reed swallowed hard, his downcast eyes told me that I'd lost one of the most wonderful people I'd ever met and a friend that I was just getting close to.

Chapter 23

"No, no, no!" I jerked away from Kento when he reached out to me. I marched the short distance over the blackened chasm that used to be my home. I slammed my palm against Reed's shoulder. Jasper couldn't be gone—dead—like my mom, like my dad, like anyone who got too close to me, anyone I cared about. "He's not dead, did you hear me? H-He can't be. I don't believe it."

"Then where is he?" Reed asked with the threat of anger in his voice. "You know as well as I that he'd be making some snide comment or a goofy joke if he was here."

I wrapped my arms around my middle, trying to hold myself together. "You're wrong." Tears streamed down my face. Please let him be okay and back at school. "We flashed here with magic, he could've done the same. He-He left like I told him to do."

"Jasper wouldn't leave you like that," Kento's eyes darkened and he turned away from me, body rigid like he was holding in his anger so he didn't strike out at me. "I can't believe you did this—after everything—after you knew what evil that side of magic does."

"This is all your fault." I push against Reed's chest, but he's solid and didn't move. "Why did you have to come to my school that day? You forced my mother to make me leave."

"And this is the thanks we get for trying to save your ass?" Reed spat. "You did this Zoey—you killed Jasper. So if we're passing blame around, you need to take up your share."

"Stop it." I shook my head so hard that I saw double for a moment. "No, no. If I'd stayed with her, this wouldn't h-have happened. She-she would still be alive a-and Jasper too."

"What did you do, Zoey?" his voice inflamed with fury.

"I wanted to make them pay for what they did." I swallowed hard, trying to hold onto my tears. "I thought I could make them bring back mom, thought…" my words wavered and tears blurred my vision.

"That's your problem, you don't think, ever!" he yelled. "Just jump in with no knowledge and think you can be the hero. The academy is full of powerful witches and maybe if you pulled your head out of your ass long enough you might just learn something."

His hands clenched, corded muscles twitching in his neck.

I hated his words, hated that he was so fucking close to the truth… "You don't know anything about me, and I don't need you. Don't need any of you."

I turned away, burning up, shaking, tears drenching my cheeks.

I felt like I was being ripped apart. *My mom! God, she'd*

been fearful of my magic that's why she hadn't taught me much.
And Jasper had only tried to help me.

A strangled cry escaped my lips. My mom was dead. And
Jasper too. I fold in on myself. Everything had led to this moment.
All my choices. The tarot had been set in granite. I couldn't have
stopped this, not even if I could reverse time, it would end the
same. And I couldn't fight the dark mages without opening myself
up the darkness too. It was so seductive. Even now in my misery
and with my heart retched into, it called to me. Beckoned me to let
it out again.

"Maybe I'm not cut out for all this magic." I sniffed. "That
all this trouble is my doing. If I didn't have any magic—was just a
regular girl, a human—my mom, Jasper, even my dad would still
be alive."

Kento avoided my gaze, the look of disappointment etched
in his face cut me deeper than any sword.

"Take the magic from me." I stared from Kento to Reed. "I-
I don't want it anymore."

"We can't do that, it will kill you." Kento glared.

"I don't care. I don't want this pain anymore. I don't want to
feel anything."

"You're giving up?" Reed shook his head as if disgusted.
"Just like that? Your mom told me that you were a fighter. That
you didn't take no or can't for answers. What would she think
now, Zoey?"

I didn't answer him, couldn't, I could only squeezed my eyes shut as tears spilled down my cheeks.

"That you let these evil bastards win? That Jasper's and her life were for nothing?" Reed continued with a razor-sharp edge to his voice. "When I first met you, I never guessed you for a quitter. I saw you take down that wraith—you were on the brink of death—yet you never stopped fighting, never faltered."

"—different." My response stuck in my throat. "It wasn't the same as this."

"Bullshit. You have the power inside you. I'm not talking about the dark magic, I'm talking about real power that none of us have seen anything like it. That's what blew up the wraith. That's the potential you have inside you that you haven't even tapped into."

"How?" I asked, desperate for any thread of hope where I had nothing but a bleak void. "I don't know how to do that, not without dark magic taking over me."

"I don't know." He shook his head, tears glistening in his eyes. "But we need to get back to the academy before more of these suckers come, cause I can't promise that I wouldn't turn dark just to rip their spines out."

"Okay," I said on a shaky breath. "Let's go back."

I wanted to believe him with everything I had left in me, but I didn't think this would work. I had to try. If it came down to me taking out the dark sorcerers responsible, I would court that darkness myself. But this time, I'd shield my men. I'd force Kento and Reed to safety. I wasn't going to lose anyone else. Not ever again.

Chapter 24

I don't even remember the ride back to the academy. We piled into Reed's car. I laid down in the backseat feeling lost, alone, and completely empty. Tears streamed down my face onto the seat like they would never end.

I was a raging inferno of grief and fury.

It was evening by the time we rolled into the school's parking lot. Not saying a word, I went straight to my dorm room. There, I locked myself in, not even caring if Kento or Reed guarded me. They were both right. If it wasn't for me, Jasper would be alive and my mom. I doubled over, pain shooting through my middle. If it wasn't for me, my mom wouldn't have been attacked, she'd be safe. I huddled on the floor. Not feeling the strength to move or do anything but cry.

When sunlight peeked through my window, I still didn't get up, I only folded in on myself wishing I could take away all this pain.

Sometime later knocks sounded on my door, but I didn't acknowledge them. Muffled words came and went.

That evening, I forced myself up and sipped water from the faucet. I turned the shower on, hoping the water would wash away some of this sorrow and anguish. I undressed and stepped inside the shower. For a long time, I sat as the water poured over me. But the water did nothing but make fresh tears burn my eyes.

For the next two days, all I drank was tap water and lay in bed, crying into my pillow until it was soaked. Or screaming until my voice was hoarse until I was numb. I felt utterly alone.

Night darkened my room and I rolled over in my bed. Wondering if I could do a death spell to take out all those responsible for my mom and Jasper's death, including myself.

A bang sounded on my door. They'd leave just like they had the past few days. But the knock came again, louder.

"Go away," I yelled.

"Open the door, Zoey," Reed's voice boomed through the door and I flinched.

What was he going to do? Hurt me? He couldn't do any more damage than I'd already suffered. "No."

"If you don't open this door, I will rip it off the hinges."

I stomped to the door, throwing it open to find him and Kento standing there. Both of their eyes were bloodshot.

"When did you last eat?" he asked, his voice softening a touch.

I didn't need their pity, I needed my mom and Jasper back. In answer I shrugged.

"Come on, we got something for you." Kento gestured. He looked thinner, paler than when I'd seen him last.

"No thanks, I'm good." I started to shut the door when Reed blocked it with his boot.

"I thought you were a fighter, Zoey. This reeks of someone who's given up."

"Yeah, well, so what." I strained against the door to close it, but it didn't move an inch. "Look I know I made a horrible mistake. T-That my actions got Jasper," my voice caught on his name, "killed, but I don't need you two reminding me or harassing me. I get it. Okay. I fucked up. I'm sorry... I should've listened to you and not gone—" I closed my eyes, fighting back tears. Tears did nothing.

"It's my fault too," Reed whispered. "I knew you were upset and worried about your mom and I should've stuck by you."

I opened my eyes, glancing from him to Kento.

"We've made our peace with what happened," Kento bowed his head. "But this isn't the answer. Starving yourself and wasting away is a slap in the face of both Jasper and your mother's memory. Honor them. Fight."

"I don't know how. I thought I did, but not anymore."

"Come with us to the cafeteria. We need to work out a plan on how to get these fuckers back." Reed held out his hand.

I took it, the warmth and contact a balm to me. He and Kento led me down the cafeteria. Part of me wanted to wrap myself around both of them, cry for everything and everyone I'd lost, but they were right. It was time to turn my sorrow into anger and avenge my mom and Jasper's death.

My stomach rumbled and Kento pushed a bag of French fries and a chocolate shake into my hands.

"Eat," he instructed.

"I-I don't think I can." I felt light-headed, queasy.

"You used a lot of magic battling and haven't eaten since," Reed's voice was all business again like before. "Even using black magic has its costs and it'll take the energy from somewhere."

I sat down but didn't touch the food as I placed them on the table. Kento opened the bag and laid out the fries on a napkin.

"And what would Jasper do if he were here?" Kento asked, sitting across from me. His eyes still held that coldness from earlier.

Before I could break down in a fresh set of tears, he popped a fry in his mouth.

"He'd steal your food. We must prepare for the next battle and avenge him. Don't let them win."

Reed didn't say anything. But he didn't need to. His anger and grief rolled off him in never-ending waves.

I stared at the fries, my mouth watering, but my soul grieving.

Reed pulled the bag closer to me. "You don't have to eat the whole bag. A few…Jasper will be smiling from Heaven that we're remembering him with his favorite thing in the world…French fries and shakes."

Reluctantly, I put one of the fries in my mouth. It was still warm and soft. Chewing it made me want another despite how I felt.

"Good, girl." Reed clinked his shake cup to mine. "To Jasper!"

"Kanpai-Cheers!" Kento shouted and touched his cup to Reed's then mine.

Caught up in the spirit and thinking that Jasper really might be smiling down on us, I did the same. "Cheers." Then took a sip. The chocolate syrup was divine. "Damn, this is good."

"Yup, Jasper's favorite." Reed stole another fry.

"Hey, those are mine." I elbowed him and he grunted, but he popped the fry into his mouth anyway.

I didn't feel any better about my mom or Jasper. All I'd done was let go of a bit of the sorrow for their memory and to comfort Kento and Reed. Through everything, I was learning, I needed to keep my friends far away and protected and draw my enemy to me.

As soon as I was able, I feigned needing to study tarot to go the library.

"I'll order you a deck online. The human versions are better than nothing," Kento offered.

Since my return, the whole school had heard about Jasper's death. Those who were on the fence about me now fully sided against me. Reed discovered the message on my bathroom mirror and told Headmistress Olsen, arguing that he'd known her for years and we had to get someone in charge involved. She had the whole school on lockdown. No one was allowed in or out. She'd blamed Jasper's death on a magic teleportation spell gone askew, but the glares I got for the next two days said they knew it was my fault.

Every night, I cried myself to sleep. Every night, either Kento or Reed just held me until I fell asleep. Their arms around me and soft words bringing me a little bit of peace. And every night, I dreamed about my mom or Jasper. His crooked grin and bright eyes. The way he never seemed to take anything seriously. How he was the exact opposite of Kento, but how I'd been growing to love them the same despite all of that. How Reed was the balance between the two and how he was strong and leader material but let Kento and Jasper call the shots sometimes. A fresh wave of grief plowed into me, but I pushed back the tears.

"I don't even think the school will allow packages inside." I offered him a brittle smile. "But thanks for the thought. The library has cards I can borrow, and I wanted to check out their books too."

Kento bowed his head slightly and opened the library door for me. Inside, a waft of old books, leather and paper greeted me. God, I loved that scent and had missed it since coming to this school.

"The tarot section is over there." Reed pointed to the third set of bookshelves.

When he started to walk with me, I placed my hand on his arm. "I kinda would like to look alone."

"Zoey—"

I placed a finger over his mouth. "I promise I'll be careful, and I'll call out if there's any trouble. But come on, this is a library, what can happen?"

He gently grasped my hand and kissed the fingertip that pressed against his lips. "I'll be right over there, reading."

A cluster of thick velvet chairs drew my attention. I would give anything in the world to be able to grab a book and join him, but I had a mission. I had to find a truth-seeking spell. I had to find a way to ease this grief that followed me everywhere, that lived in my skin, that kept my heart from beating fully.

"I'll see you in a bit." I squeezed his hand once then slipped away to the bookshelves. For a few minutes, I opened a random book or two as I could feel Kento's gaze on me. But soon he got lulled into the safety of the book in his hands and the cozy, quietness of the library.

Swiftly, I moved to the other shelves, hunting for a book of spells. One that would allow me to start questioning students to see if they knew who the dark mages were or if they were one. I would need to test it out though, to make sure it worked. But I couldn't sit around doing nothing. Waiting for the evil to attack. I hadn't even begun my recompense on them for what they did to my mother and Jasper.

My fingers trailed over the book titles: *Brewing better potions, Transmutation spells,* someone had even shoved a tiny, red book of love spells that was marked up with notes in purple ink between the books. That would be classified as dark magic if it overtook the will of another. I shook my head, but pushed it back in its place. Who was I to judge?

I went to the next aisle, but that one was all about magical history. The other shelves held books in languages I couldn't read. I let out a sigh, about to give up, when a black book with golden pages caught the light.

Looking right and left to ensure Kento hadn't come searching for me, I pulled the book down. It was a small thing, like the love spells had been. But its pages gleamed in the fluorescent light and I had to know what was inside.

Flipping it open, spell after spell in English flashed at me. And near the front was one on discovering the truth. *Jackpot.*

"Zoey?" Kento's whisper sent a shiver down my spine.

I stuffed the book in my backpack, schooling my features as I dashed around the side. He wouldn't approve of what I was going to do. But I didn't care. I had to know who at the school was guilty and enact my judgment.

His pinched brow softened when he saw me. "I thought you

took off."

"Nope. I'm right here."

"Did you find a tarot deck or book you want to get?"

"Uh, yeah, sure." I hustled over to the appropriate shelf and snatched up the first random book and box of cards I found. "These ones."

"The Traveler's Tarot?" He frowned down at it. "I thought you'd get a more modern one like the Celtic Dragon or Cosmic Phoenix."

I shrugged a shoulder. "They remind me of my mom."

That evening, I pretended to be asleep. Not that I ever slept well since my mom and Jasper's death. I stifled a cry. *Think of the end result, of those who did this dead.* When Reed started lightly snoring next to me, I wiggled free of his grasp, my heart pounding that he'd wake up and stop me.

I dug the spell book from my backpack and went into the bathroom. Even though Kento had washed off the message, I still felt it there. Could retrace the letters and exactly where they were placed.

Using my phone as I light, I turned to the truth-seeking page and whispered the spell.

"Make my enemies known, by breath and bone. Let the truth

be shown, by the moonlight and rowan. Bring the truth out of the shadows and make them glow."

I repeated the spell, tracing my fingers on the mirror, imagining the letters that had been there.

The streaks left by my fingertip illuminated and I gasped. It worked. Now all I had to do was find out who had written this message and who the others were in their evil group.

Chapter 25

For the third time, I repeated the spell, as I stared at the words on the mirror my fingertip had made: *We're coming for you.* Willing them to reveal their secrets to me. My magic buzzing across my palms and impromptu, I placed them on the mirror.

The image of me and my bathroom wavered. Suddenly it was Megan standing in my bathroom, black goo on her fingertip as she wrote the message.

That bitch! I slammed my hand down on the counter.

"Zoey?" Reed called out groggily.

"Just using the bathroom." I rushed out. My heart pounding, I shoved the book in my backpack and wiped down the mirror. Any second I was sure Reed was going to stumble in and catch me, but he didn't. I slid back into bed, knowing if I didn't, he'd wake up all the way.

For hours, I laid wake, Megan's name pounding against the back of my skull. When I was sure that Reed was back asleep, I got out of bed and quietly got ready. I was going after Megan and I'd make her tell me who all was in their group. Had my magic known that she was guilty? Was that why it had lashed out that day with the match and Jasper?

Just thinking about him sent a fresh blade sinking into my chest and I blinked back tears.

I snuck out of my room, not wanting to wake Reed. Neither he nor Kento would approve of what I'd done or what I was about to do.

The hallways were dark as I made my way to the other side of the girl's dorms. I had no idea which room Megan was in, but the magic truth spell would tell me. One at a time, I laid my hand on a door and recited the spell: "Make my enemies known, by breath and bone. Let the truth be shown, by the moonlight and rowan. Bring the truth out of the shadows and make them glow."

Nothing. I moved to the next door and repeated the process. It wasn't until the eighth door that my hand felt burning hot. I lifted my palm off the wood and my handprint glowed in the dim light. *Bingo.*

I knocked on the door and when no one answered, I banged against the wood. There would be no hiding from me. I would find her if she wasn't in her room and drag her to justice.

"Who is it?" she called out in a sleepy voice.

I only knocked louder.

"For fuck's sake," she yelled, throwing open the door.

I didn't give her time to slam the door in my face but pushed inside. Her room was the same size as mine, but had a plush-looking bed, pictures on the walls, and a shelf overloaded with statues, knickknacks, and books.

"Wha—get out of my room!" She stomped her foot.

"Why did you write that message on my mirror?" I spun, facing her.

She blanched, then shook her head. "You're insane. I didn't do anything, now get out of my room."

I crossed the distance between us, and she flinched back like I'd struck her. A tiny whimper sounded from her throat. I grasped her wrist and she tried to jerk away from me.

"Make my enemies known, by breath and bone. Let the truth be shown, by the moonlight and rowan. Bring the truth out of the shadows and make them glow," I said.

"Ow! You're hurting me!"

I dropped her arm and pointed. "It's glowing, Megan. And the spell showed me that you wrote that message on my mirror. You and your sick friends are responsible for Jasper's death and my mom's and I'm here to pass judgment on your ass." I pushed aside the logic that Jasper was my fault as I went on a tangent and used my power, smoldering him and the other mages.

"No, no!" she screamed, holding up her hands. "It wasn't m-me...I didn't do anything."

My magic skidded across my palms, sparking.

"I-I mean, yes, I w-wrote the message." She backed up against the far wall.

"Give me names. Who is a dark mage?"

She stared down at her arm, which still glowed where my

hand had touched her.

"It's a truth-seeking spell." I smirked, holding onto my magic until she gave me what I wanted. "You can't lie."

"I don't know any dark mages except you." She lifted her chin. "Because of you, I will have scars for the rest of my life. My stupid astral spirit is forever connected to yours."

"Tell me who hurt Jasper! Tell me who hurt my mom!"

She crumpled, holding her arms over her head. "I-I don't know!"

"You have to know, you wrote the fucking message, Megan. Tell me!" I clenched my fists, the magic in my palms lashing against my flesh to be free.

"Alright, yes, I wrote the message." She peered at me through her arms covering her head. "But only to scare you. To get you to want to leave the academy."

I didn't believe her.

"It's true! I can't lie remember, because of your spell. I only wanted you gone, nothing more."

"Then—then who are the dark mages? Who killed my mom and Jasper?"

"D-Do a truth spell on the school! Find out that way."

How? Most hated me anyway and this way I could prove Jasper wasn't entirely my fault. That the dark mages were ultimately responsible.

I withdrew my magic and it scraped against my flesh, angry

at not being used. Swallowing down the bile in the back of my throat, I went to her door. "You may not have done this, but your actions helped sway the scale for me wanting to go check on my mom. So indirectly, like me, you are responsible for Jasper's death. One way or another, you will pay."

I swung her door open to leave, when she called out.

"He's not dead."

Chapter 26

Had I heard her right? Who wasn't dead? Jasper? My heart swelled with hope and tears stung the back of my eyes.

I looked over my shoulder at her.

She'd lowered her arms, my handprint still glowed. Maybe she'd done a counterspell or something when I was leaving.

"Jasper," she licked her lips. "He's not dead. Th-The dark mages have him."

I raced over to her, crouching in front of her and her eyes widened in fright. "If you are lying to me, I will kill you with my bare hands. No magic. Just me."

"It's true, I swear it," she rushed out.

"How? How is that you know this if you're not one of them?"

"W-We're connected right?" Her voice shook. "They've been sending messages. Nightmares, really. Since the day you left, I've been having them in my head. I can't get rid of them. I can't sleep."

I ground my back teeth. "What did they say? What do they want?"

"You." She blinked and tears rolled down her cheeks. "They

say they'll exchange Jasper for you."

"How?" I gripped her arm and she winced.

"At midnight. I-I'll write the spell they want you to do to c-call them."

Seeing the pain in her eyes, I let go of her. "Sorry. Write down everything you can remember."

"What are you going to do?" she asked.

I hadn't been able to save my mom. That raw wound would never heal. I carried it in my heart and the fact I'd failed her would be with me forever. But I could punish those who had done this to her and save another innocent life. "I'm going to bring back Jasper."

"No, it's a trap." Reed raked a hand through his silver hair. "You have to know that, right?"

"I do." I lined up the ingredients for the spell. A sprig of witch-hazel, a rowan berry, a seashell. The latter I borrowed from Megan. Saltwater, which I had to improvise and use tap water and table salt. A feather, which I got from Kento as one of his swords had a feather drawn on the sheath, a stick of incense, and a candle along with Jasper's matchbox.

"If Jasper is alive, he wouldn't want you to do this," Kento argued.

Both he and Reed paced around me. Neither knew better than to try and stop me. I would do whatever it took to bring Jasper back. Part of me hoped that they had my mom alive too, but Megan hadn't said anything about that. Right now, I had to get Jasper back, then I could think about finding Mom if she was still alive. All three of my men could help me get her back if she was kidnapped like Jasper had been.

"I've gone over every argument you two are doing now in my head. This is the only way."

"It's almost midnight, we need to go." Kento handed me my book bag so I could load all the supplies inside.

"You're helping her with this madness?" Reed asked, his face twisted up in disbelief.

"Yes. She will do this regardless. Better she has us on her side." Kento touched my shoulder. "Do you remember what to do? And the magic words we went over?"

I nodded. They had been so hard to pronounce, to memorize, but Kento and I had practiced them for hours while Reed helped gather up the supplies we'd needed.

"Shit. Fine." Reed grabbed his shoes from under my bed. "But no sacrificing, Zoey. We get Jasper back and we hit them with all our might."

I nodded. I didn't care about what happened to me, but I wanted to see Jasper again, I wanted these bastards to pay for what they did.

My bag banged against my side as I marched with Kento on my right and Reed on my left to the football field and the spot where the wraith had exploded. The grass hadn't grown here, it was a black patch like when it had first happened. Strange, as I'd have figured in an academy full of magic users that they'd have cleared this up by now with some spell.

I set out the items in a circle just inside the scorched grass. Then we stood in the circle. I nodded to Kento, who drew out his katana, the one that had a matching feather to the shaft etched on the handle. In slow motion, he slid the blade across my palm. I hissed out a breath. The steel felt cold and my blood bubbled up.

"I call the dark mages!" I let my blood hit the center of the circle, reciting the spell Megan had given me. "I offer my life in exchange for Jasper."

Wind whistled through the trees in the nearby forest. They swayed as though some invisible giant was passing through them to us.

When the wind blasted through us, the candle flame flickered and went out. We were plunged into darkness.

"I'll get the light," Reed said, and struck a match.

At the edge of our circle was Jasper, bound and gagged with half a dozen hooded mages standing around him.

"Jasper!" My heart strangled in my throat. He was alive! Maybe there was a chance that my mom was too. I gave a nod to Jasper, then to Kento and Reed.

If this didn't work out how we planned, then we'd call for help. Get Olsen involved. But I had already discerned that the more people we brought to this meeting, the less chance we had of getting Jasper back. The dark sorcerers were cowards. They wouldn't want to face off against an entire school or the faculty. No, we had to keep this personal and private for now.

"Do you willingly exchange yourself for Jasper?" one of them said, pushing Jasper a step forward.

"I do. Let us exchange places. He, to the center of the circle with Reed and Kento, and me with you."

The man holding Jasper grunted then shoved him forward. Jasper's green eyes met mine and he shook his head. I knew what he'd say if he wasn't gagged. He'd tell me not to do this. To save myself.

I straightened my spine and my resolve and kissed him on the cheek before I passed and took his place.

His muffled scream tore my heart, but I kept walking.

Two of the closest mages grabbed my arms. I looked over my shoulder, Reed and Kento were trying to keep Jasper from running at me. They whispered words in his ears that I hoped would soothe his pain some.

As I neared the edge of the circle, I stumbled, falling to the ground. I pressed my bloody palm to the grass and let the herbs and salt in my other hand fall on top.

"Ego in hoc circulo inimicus!" I shouted and a circle within a circle rose up.

I felt their shock as they glanced around, trying in vain to teleport, to leave the circle. Since they had had spies at the school, we used that to our advantage. It was common knowledge that I didn't know the magical spell language, so they hadn't expected me to be able to trap them in a circle. They were stuck with me and my three guys were safe, shielded in their own circle.

Reed's jaw was set. He had the magic talisman to beckon others to help us if we needed. His human cell phone wouldn't work in a magical circle.

And I'd asked him for this. For the chance to do this on my own, but he was ready to summon help.

"Foolish bitch!" the mage holding my arm yanked me up. "Do you think this changes anything? That you've stopped us? We don't want you, we want the magic inside of you—that created you."

Before I could ask what he was talking about, he yanked me by my hair and threw me to the ground. My hip took the impact and I rolled to my feet.

Suddenly, his power jerked me up into the air like a giant fist clutched me. I choked out a breath as my throat constricted. I couldn't breathe.

"Zoey!" Before Kento could take a step, he was thrown backward. He hit an invisible wall, blood coating his face.

No! I thrashed, tried to get free to help him. But the invisible grip only tightened. I fought for air as spots danced before my vision. Fought to bring my magic forward.

Reed loosened his spell, lighting it on fire.

Help was coming.

I clawed at the unseen force that squeezed my throat.

"Did you think you could best us with your puny magic?" He sneered in my face. "It's pathetic. You could've been so great. We'd have worshipped you, made you our queen as you were destined to be."

I wanted to spit in his hooded face. I wanted to tell him to go fuck himself, but I couldn't get any more words to come out. Once more, I tried to use my magic. My power sizzled across my palms. Yes!

The mage laughed and the others mimicked the sound. Their power joining his and the magic I'd been able to draw sputtered out.

Terror snaked down my spine.

We still had another chance. Reed's spell would've reached Olsen, the other faculty members and the entire school. Calling whoever wanted to come fight to do so. I just had to hold on a little longer.

"I'm going to enjoy ripping the dark magic from you," the mage whispered, his voice sending my body into tremors.

He stretched out his hand to me, speaking in a language that sounded like how demons might talk. "Klubreg, mxul amrebre sacrarea."

Pain cleaved my chest. A scream ripped through the air and I realized it wasn't mine. Megan stood on the outside of the circle, her hand clutching her heart. *Oh shit! If I died, so did she.* I hadn't thought about that. I'd only thought about getting Jasper back.

Behind her, Olsen and a dozen teachers dashed out of school in their pajamas and robes. Several students came too, but not everyone. Can't say that I blamed them.

A fresh stab struck me again, and I couldn't breathe as pain vibrated through my entire body.

The teachers and a handful of students raised their hands or wands and started reciting spells. But the mage's cloaks glimmered in the moonlight, none of them falling, none of them stopping.

"Too bad you wouldn't taste the darkness that we offer." The mage lowered his hood.

His eyebrows and hair were gone. But his face and the memories of him flooded my mind. The bully who terrorized kids at school...the one I had put a spell on that burned him. *Darren!*

I shook my head, choking on blood that bubbled up in my throat at another wrenching pain that sent me crashing down to my knees. "No, no...you're human. You can't have magic."

"See that's where you're wrong. I was recruited Freshman year by the dark mages, and I was undercover at the school. Once you did your prank on me, I was able to trace the magic back to you. I came to your house to confront you when I saw you leaving with those three bastards." He nodded his head over at Jasper, Kento, and Reed. "Together, we trailed you to this place and that's when we did a spell to make everyone think we were part of the student body and slipped right in unnoticed."

"You released that wraith, didn't you? Made it stronger."

"That's the beauty of dark magic, it is always stronger than the light." He flicked his hand and searing pain shot through my chest.

The edges of my vision dimmed as I gasped, trying to draw in a breath, but only finding a vacuum that sucked my soul out bit by bit. I gritted my teeth. Tried to fight. "Guess you're not so strong," I spat out a mouthful of blood. "Can't get your hair to grow back? You let a non-trained witch like me show you up."

He punched me in the gut, and I doubled over. His power lashing across my skin.

Muscles grew weaker.

"This is where I win, and you are a loser like you've always been." He bent down, pushing my sweaty hair out of my face. Then he punched me again and a searing pain broke across my side. My scream filled the night.

Oh god, I'm gonna die.

"Zoey!" Reed cried. He, Jasper, and Kento rammed their shoulders into the invisible circle that separated them from me.

Outside our double circle, the mages were sending spells and dark magic that ripped through the few that had come to help us fight. Megan lay on the ground, writhing in pain. Blood streaming from her chest, her face pale, her scars from the fire making gray streaks across half her face and neck. The other teachers and Olsen weren't fairing much better. The Headmistress' hair was plastered to her head. She held one arm to her side, and I blanched at seeing the flesh nearly torn off it.

"And your stupid magic circle?" He leaned down, yanking my hair back. "Once I have your magic, your circle will fall. And I'll rip the magic from your three boyfriends just like I did your mom. I should thank her though, it's because of her that I'm now a dark mage."

Sounds around me faded. My vision tunneled onto his gloating face.

"Don't think to out-magic me, Zoey." Darren shook his head. "You will lose against me cause that's all you've ever been, a loser. It's even more evident here among those with power. You had all this potential and you refused to use it."

He stood, the invisible force slamming into me so hard that my body jerked. Tears streamed down my face as I fought once more. Fought to do something. Fought for my power. Fought for my life. Colors around me spun into grays and blacks while my power leaked out of me in dark streams and into Darren.

I convulsed. The image of this monster hurting my mom burned inside me. I held on to the magic leaving me with everything I had left.

Cries sounded in the distance. They seemed so far.

Flares of magic from others burst at the corners of my vision but none of it stopped the mages or Darren.

I tried to scream, choking on blood as it filled my mouth.

My vision dimmed. Sorrow slammed into me that I'd failed everything. Failed this new school. Failed my magic. Failed my mom. Failed Jasper, Kento and Reed. I had no doubt that Darren and these others would do exactly what they said. They'd steal their magic and kill them.

A rumbling vibrated around me, pulsing the air, matching each slow beat of my heart. I'd felt this before. With the wraith. But it slipped faster than I could grasp it.

Darren flinched back. "You won't win! I'm more powerful than you! Dark magic is stronger than light."

He shoved an inky black magic at me that covered me. It stuck to every part of me and felt like it was yanking out my soul.

Power flared inside my chest hard and fast. It felt like a tug-of-war inside me. That each time I slipped a fraction, another sliver of my soul was cleaved away. The thought of Jasper, Kento and Reed suffering, dying—I had to do this. Even if I died in the process. I needed to stop these monsters from hurting anyone else.

Searing pain rushed forward, bowing my back. Heat surged throughout every cell of my being. I screamed without sound. I was being burned alive from the inside out.

Then the magic blasted out of me with an explosion. The

power ripped from me and into everyone in the circle. Even my three guys were blown outside their protection.

Chapter 27

"She's waking up," Jasper's voice echoed in my ears.

I smiled, then groaned, cause even that small movement hurt like hell. But I wanted to see him. Touch him. Ensure myself that he was whole and well, that they all were. So I forced my eyes open a crack.

Jasper stood over me, Kento beside him. Kento had a cast on his arm and I gasped.

"It's okay," he touched my hand gently, "I'll have my sword arm back in no time, you'll see."

"Magic?" I croaked out. Why hadn't he healed it using a spell?

He looked at Jasper, then back at me. "Our magic is crippled right now. Don't worry, it's coming back slowly, but there's people who were in the fight that are worse off than me. I can wait a few months for my arm to heal naturally."

Where was Reed? I couldn't turn my neck and gestured to Jasper.

"Hey, thanks for saving me." He leaned down and brushed his lips across mine. "Though, next time can you not do it on such a grand gesture? I mean, you made that freaking circle take up half the football field."

I chuckled, but gasped as fresh pain lanced up my side. "Where's Reed?"

"Right here." A shuffling sounded and Reed hobbled around on crutches. "Don't worry, it's just a fractured ankle. Nurse Jenkins said it would heal in a few weeks."

"Let me." I pushed up against the pillows, only now realizing I had a neck brace on, which explained why I couldn't turn my head far. "I've got that spell book and am getting better, I can heal—"

"No," Reed and Kento said in unison.

"Why not?" I pouted. "The magic circles I created worked and I defeated the dark mages, right?"

"You got lucky." Reed leaned down on his crutches, touching my hand. "There's still a lot for you to learn about magic about your power. Hell, I don't even know how you did what you did. Nothing should be able to cut through a magical sphere like you did."

My blush heated my cheeks. "But you are all okay? Really?"

I couldn't believe it. I was the luckiest girl in the world, in the universe. Except, my mom wasn't here to share this with. A fresh wave of grief slammed into me. She hadn't deserved to die, to have her magic ripped out of her.

"Yeah," Jasper said, something flashed in his eyes, but he

blinked at it was gone. "You saved us."

He leaned down and kissed me again, making my mind turn to mush. His lips ripped off mine as Reed nudged him aside.

"My turn." He sat on the bed, Kento holding his crutches for him. "Zoey, we can't thank you enough for saving us."

"Well, it was because of me that you all were in this mess." Guilt making a ball of regret press against my heart.

"Regardless. You could've saved yourself. Could've offered to join the dark mages—you didn't know if you could defeat them or not—Hell, our own Headmistress and staff couldn't scratch them. I just want to say thank you. I'm sorry I didn't trust you. If I believed in your more, Jasper might not have taken you by himself. I'm sorry."

I reached up and cupped his face. "It's not your fault, but I forgive you. And I'll trust you to listen to me and for us work together in the future."

He leaned down, breathing me in, then kissed me slowly, gently, like I was a fragile, precious treasure he was afraid of breaking. Pleasure rolled through me, making me breathless.

"Alright, that's enough." Kento snapped his crutches at him.

"Sorry about your arm." I swallowed against the lump of emotions clogging my throat. "Wait, where's Megan? Is she okay?"

He nodded. "She's in the infirmary, feels about the same as you is my guess, but she's alive."

I breathed out a sigh of relief. Didn't want any innocent lives on my hands, even if she did hate me, she didn't deserve to die because of it.

Mom would be proud of me for being the better person. I imagined she looked down on me from above. My heart twisted and I brushed back tears. She would want me to live my life despite her death. To make it right in other ways like helping others. Like not letting the evil bastards turn my heart to stone. And I had a feeling that these three guys could help me do that.

Kento leaned down and I held my breath, wondering if he would kiss me like the others had. He'd never kissed me before. Would our first kiss be in front of Jasper and Reed?

He inched down further, and my pulse sped up as I stared at his mouth. His breath fanned my face, sending shivers through me. But then he changed direction, like he thought better of it, and pressed his lips to my forehead.

As much as it hurt, I couldn't stop smiling. I was alive. So were Kento and Reed and we had Jasper back.

My heart still ached about my mom and all I'd lost. I wanted to make her proud of me and show everyone that I could do this. That I could learn how to harness and control my magic without crossing over into evil like the dark mages.

If Mom had trained me to do magic, maybe we wouldn't be here now. Maybe my life might be completely different now.

I had to move forward. Had to honor my mom for teaching

me not to be a quitter no matter how much it hurt. I didn't think that the pain in me from her death, of not getting to say goodbye or hugging her one last time, will ever fade. Not that I wanted it to. I wanted to remember her and what happened to her.

I wanted to hold her memory close to my heart forever.

And how I almost lost Jasper because of rushing in and taking the easy way out. Darren had said that light magic was weak. He was wrong. It took a whole hell of a lot of strength to do what was right, to not let the darkness inside me to win. And I hope I'm up to the task.

Coming Soon!

Last time evil came, it left mayhem and sorrow in its wake.

What will be the costs this second time around?

Zoey has made it through her first semester of Magic Academy, barely. Still reeling from her losses, she realizes she doesn't quite fit into this school either. While she hunts for those responsible for killing her parents, she uncovers more riddles and secrets.

Her relationship with the three 'hot' guys grows more complicated, including that one might not have escaped the dark mages unscathed. But can she really trust any of them?

As tough as her training and classwork are, she must learn how to control her powers before the dark mages strike again and her new world comes crashing down. Except that even her own magic fights against her to give up the rules and go for blood. If she does, she'll become an enemy of the light and her guys.

Can she juggle three guys, new magical classes, and the battles to come?

Welcome to the Magic Guardian Academy where supernatural creatures try to keep the world safe even on the days that suck.

Warning: This is a steamy reverse harem paranormal romance that will leave you addicted.

About the Author

Rebecca Goodwin fell in love with fairytales and sword fighting. Now, she creates damsels-in-distress that rescue themselves and often the heroes.

When not creating fantasy worlds and characters, Rebecca enjoys singing along to the radio and maintaining her fencing practice which she teaches to her son and daughter. Rebecca lives in Boston with her husband, two kids, three cats and three dogs. She loves hearing from readers.

Signup to her VIP Newsletter today:

http://eepurl.com/cWQ3gv

UnderLand series:

Underland - Book 1

Fairest - Book 2

Puppet Maker - Book 3

Submerge - Book 3

Olympian Elemental Trails series:

Hidden Legacy - Book 1

Fated Quest - Book 2

Sneak Peek

My best friend was trying to kill me. I clutched the evidence of what would cause a would-be heart attack in my fist and marched into her house.

Rock music vibrated against my chest and rattled Emily's windows. With nods and hellos, I pressed through the crowd deeper into the house, tossing my high school graduation gown along with the others on a recliner. People danced to the music while others mingled. It was mid-afternoon, but the party wouldn't stop until dawn. The scent of tobacco and perfume clogged my throat.

"Congrats!" Tim, my old high school crush, winked with his arm around his girlfriend. He was already in college.

"Thanks." I turned from him, scanning the area for Emily. A prickly sensation hit the back of my neck and I spun. There was a guy leaning against the wall staring at me. His eyes seemed to glow. I blinked to clear my vision when someone bumped into me.

"Sorry," a girl said.

I looked back for the guy with weird eyes but he was gone. My friend Beth waved at me from the other side of the room and I smiled back. But my attention shifted to finding my best friend and finding out why she wanted me dead.

I spotted Emily's brother and made a beeline to him. He'd know where she was hiding. "Congrats on graduating. Emily told me you finished your electrician certification."

"Yup." Derek grinned. His blond curls making a soft halo around his head.

Their parents always lumped their birthdays together on the same day even though they were a year and two days apart. So why would graduation be any different? "Have you seen Emily?"

"She's in the kitchen."

"Thanks. Good to see you."

He nodded and I moved past the mix of high school graduates and Derek's friends into the kitchen.

"Paige," Emily, shouted opening a soda. Her blond hair was twisted into a messy bun and she wore a sleeveless silk top that showed off her tan. "Over here."

"Hey!" I squeezed past two other classmates and waved the airline ticket at her. "What is this?"

She smiled, but her blue eyes pinched at the edges. "We talked about going to Greece months ago."

"That was speculative." I placed the ticket on the counter, afraid to pick it up again and make the trip more real. My voice was shaky, "You know I can't do this."

Her eyes widened. "You're not chickening out, are you? 'Cause you know I brought a tranquilizer gun with me." Her voice sounded on the verge of whining. "I will so tie your ass to your seat on the plane if I have to."

An uncomfortable pain laced around my middle. When I'd opened her gift on my hands shook so bad I couldn't drive for several minutes. My heart had felt like it was going to explode.

Three college girls shuffled into the kitchen and loaded up paper plates with snacks.

"Look, I know." She leaned against the counter, crossing her ankles. Her rainbow-colored shoestrings were bright against her black tennis shoes. "But it's been over two years. You deserve a break, okay?"

My folks and I were supposed to go to Europe that summer but we never did. It had been my dream to become an archeologist just like my dad and visit all the ancient ruins. Now that had been pushed aside for a business degree. How could I dig up fossils around the world if the mere idea of an airplane made me want to vomit?

"God, Emily. Are you sure we have to do this? Why can't we just hang out here?"

"No way, missy." She shook her head. "You swore you'd come with me and the others in Greek class to go to Greece. Hell, you even helped raise the most money selling those damn candles to pay for everything. You can't back out now."

I so wanted to see the Acropolis, Parthenon, Coliseum and all the ancient temples, but the idea of flying and the party music thumping sent my pulse throbbing inside my skull. My skin felt cold and clammy. "I don't think I can do this."

"Sure you can."

Beth called from the living room. "Emily! We got spilled punch on your carpet."

"Be right there." Emily grasped my elbow. "Give me a sec, we're not done talking about this." She let go with a smile and rummaged under the sink for cleaner and a rag then disappeared into the crowd.

The overwhelming sensation to run fill me. If I hurried, I could escape out the back without her knowing. I shook my head. No, that would be a cowardly thing to do and rude. What was going on with me? I felt off and not just from the fear of having to fly. Maybe I just needed some air. I walked to the kitchen's bay window, looking out onto the pool. Floating candles and flowers floated across the surface. A few people milled about but no one I recognized. Then a flash like a camera drew my attention.

That same guy from earlier stood staring at the house…at me. Goosebumps trailed along my skin. I felt drawn to him despite my heart racing like I was approaching a chasm to jump off into an abyss. Who was this guy? Did Emily know him?

Curiosity eating me up, I pushed out the backdoor and into the warm, summer evening. The scent of citronella to keep away mosquitoes was thick and I coughed. Music from inside the house was subdued to the base and a few strands of notes drifting in and out.

I glanced around searching for the guy with glowing eyes. They had to be contacts. From across the pool, I found him staring at me with his hypnotic eyes. I crossed around the pool toward him.

"Hello," I said suddenly feeling unsure. My insides curled but I couldn't move away.

"It's taken me a long time to find you." His voice sounded older than he looked.

"Oh?" I brushed my hair off my shoulder. "Are you friends with Emily's brother?"

"Come with me." He held out his hand.

I stared at his palm, my heart pounding so hard I couldn't think. My mind screaming to run but I'd no idea why. Nothing was making sense. All I could do was move forward and place my hand in his. It felt cold and a shiver ran through me.

"That's right, it will all be over soon," his voice was soothing, turning my mind to mush. "No need to get on that flight you've been dreading. Just stay here with me." Why had I hesitated in doing what he asked? He was wonderful and everything would be fine. With my hand in his, he led me out the side gate. I wouldn't have to get on an airplane, I could be with him instead.

We walked across the front yard toward a shiny, silver Tesla Roadster. When he opened the door for me, the scent of ions charging like just before a lightning storm burned my nostrils.

"Paige!" Emily shouted from the front door and charged out after us.

The guy cursed, pulling away from me. A fogginess lifted off my mind and I stumbled backward as though I was drunk or something.

"What the hell are you doing?" She yanked my arm, dragging me toward her. "Leaving with some guy you don't know just to avoid the flight?"

He chuckled but climbed into his car and sped away.

I turned to her, "Do you know him?"

"No," Emily said with a glare at the departing vehicle. "Must be a party crasher. Come back inside."

For a moment, I stared down the street where he'd vanished. A sense of foreboding pressing across my shoulders like a wet blanket.

Back inside, she gave me a hug and pushed a soda into my hands which wouldn't stop shaking. What had been up with that guy? Why had I followed him to his car? That wasn't like me at all and now that he was gone any good vibes I'd had in his presence now made my stomach heave.

"Hey, if you really want to call off this vacation, I understand. But jeez, Paige, going off with some guy you just met? He could've been a serial killer or something."

"I know." Hoping it would help, I swallowed down the soda. "I-I don't know what I was thinking."

"Hey, it's okay." She rubbed my back.

"And I am petrified of the flight." I took a shaky breath. "What if the engine fails or there's a thunderstorm over the ocean? What if we crash?" The words tumbled out of my mouth and I couldn't take a deep enough breath.

"Nothing is going to happen. I promise."

I'd signed up for a full load this summer and my courses started in two weeks. I wanted to get college over and done. Darren and Mike squeezed into the kitchen past two girls chatting.

"What's up, Paige?" Darren and Mike asked.

"Hi," I said politely.

Nothing had ever clicked with us despite their jockey good-looks. It had been hell in the movie theater with their groping hands. I swore they'd morphed into an octopus during our double date with Beth.

"If you stay, you can always keep the wonder twins company," Emily whispered in my ear as they disappeared back into the living room.

Focusing on my getting my degree was top priority. Guys were too much of a distraction. I didn't need to complicate my life right now.

"Please come with me." Emily gave me her trademark puppy-dog look that I couldn't say no to. "Listen, I stole two sleeping pills from my mom's stash. You can take one when we check-in and the other if you need it during the flight. Say you'll come. Please, please, please."

"I am so going to regret this, aren't I?"

Emily squealed. "*Yes!* Let's go before I decide to make you do something even more daring, like streak at our first college football game."

A nervous laugh broke through my lips and I shook my head. Knowing I wouldn't be able to live with myself if I broke my vow and didn't at least try.

Emily pulled out a small, blue container and handed it to me. "Here's the pills."

I shoved the small box into the pocket of my jeans. I'd tried half a dozen times over the years since my parents had died to fly. Once I even got as far as the air terminal, and that was with over a year of counseling first, but I still couldn't get past the check-in.

Emily recited the airline's safety stats while my stomach churned and I worried I was going to throw up before we even left. Fellow graduates wondered in and out of the kitchen, refilling their drinks and getting snacks from the kitchen table.

She held out her hand. "Give me your car keys."

"What…why?"

"Because I'm driving to keep you from conveniently forgetting where the airport is. Or driving like an old lady so we miss our flight."

I grumbled, but dug out my keys and handed them to her.

My stomach rolled at the thought of sitting in the airport, watching the people board and not knowing if our plane would be the one to go down as my parents' had. I could do crazy stuff and even had after their death, like cave diving, running with the bulls in Mexico, and even riding a wild stallion during a rodeo, but get on a plane and trust that I wouldn't die? Nope. I forced my mind to think of the destination: amazing, exotic Greece and not how we were getting there.

"But it's graduation," I argued. "Everyone's here for one last hoorah. Can't we go to Greece tomorrow? Or even better, we can check out that male strip club that opened up downtown. Spend our money there instead."

"No. Now come on." She dragged me out of her house while our friends wished us good luck.

Yeah. Luck. That was absent from my life. For a year, I

checked myself out of school while I grieved and didn't leave the house unless I had to. It was Emily who had argued with me that my parents would've been disappointed that I had let the crash break me. I had to take chances, which is why I finally agreed to go with her to Greece.

"What would your folks say if they knew you had this opportunity and were throwing it away?" she asked as we hiked to my car.

I twisted my brown hair in my fist over my shoulder. Anxiety sat like a frozen iceberg in my gut. She was right. They'd be distraught that I couldn't move past this. All my life they'd gone on exotic trips and we'd done fun stuff as a family. I'd stayed behind in order to attend Prom. If Mom hadn't gone I'd have at least one parent left. But she followed Dad wherever he went. Even quitting her job as a lawyer to help him dig in the dirt.

Getting my mind off flying would be better than me obsessing. "Are you going to practice your Greek when we get there?"

"Hell, no." She flipped her blond curls over her shoulder. "You know, statistically, we've got a better chance of dying in a car wreck than on a plane."

"That totally doesn't help me feel any better." I opened the passenger side of my car and climbed inside. "Where's your suitcase"

"Daniel's bringing them with him. He'll meet us at the

terminal." She started my old Mustang and drove down the street. "We're only going to be gone six days. And I have yours from last month when I helped you packed."

Right, Daniel. Her boyfriend she'd met in Greek class was going with us and the other members in her class. Emily had insisted I get my suitcase ready early and taken it with her weeks ago, which I'd forgotten until she mentioned it. As my best friend, she knew me better than I knew myself, because I hadn't even thought of packing with all the fear pumping through my veins. That must have been why I nearly went with that guy at the party. My phobia making me chose what it perceived as an escape from flying.

"God, why do airport sections have to be called terminals?" I leaned back in my seat. "Shouldn't we get a ride to the airport so we don't have to pay for parking?"

"Stop trying to stall." She pursed her lips. "My dad and Derek are going to come pick up the car tomorrow morning."

I slumped in the passenger seat. Would the sleeping pill really help? I still wasn't ready to jump on a plane. No, I had a feeling a dozen pills wouldn't do the trick, either. My head swam in a mix of apprehension and the start of a weird headache.

As we rounded the corner, the guy from the party appeared in the middle of the road.

"Watch out!" I screamed.

Emily slammed on the brakes and any calmness I had fled as

we fishtailed.

"What the hell was that? Are you trying to get us in an accident?"

I searched behind us for his body. Had we missed him? There wasn't anything in the road. "Didn't you see the guy in the middle of the road?"

"What? No. God, Paige, you scared the shit out of me." She righted the car and we continued toward the airport.

Every fiber in my being screamed at me to go back home and not come out again.

"Stop freaking out, Paige." She gave me a sidelong glance like she was worried I'd lost my mind and maybe I was. "Nothing is going to happen. I promise."

I fiddled with my seatbelt strap, clutching the material as sweat trickled down my back.

"Dad paid for an upgrade on our tickets. First-class, so we'll be whisked on before anyone else. That way we can board, you take the pill, and fall asleep before we take off."

We took the airport exit and a jet bellowed overhead. *Shit!* My fingernails dug into the armrest. *This was really happening. Oh, God!*

By the time she pulled into a parking space, I was hyperventilating. Spots danced before my eyes.

"I can't do this." I panted. "I'm sorry…I just…I can't."

Emily unhooked her seatbelt and took one of my hands in

hers. "What did you make me promise when we agreed to this?"

My vision tunneled to a pinprick and I couldn't focus on what she was saying. My chest grew tighter with each breath.

She squeezed my hand gently. "Four months ago, when I asked if you would come with me to Greece, what did you say?"

I blinked, my eyelids were so heavy I struggled to open them. My whole body felt like I was encased in cement. I felt weird...*off*. My mouth dried and my tongue was too thick. What was happening to me? "You told to help you get on that plane. Whatever it took. That you'd hate yourself forever if you didn't go to Greece."

Numbness slithered across my body.

"Remember what we swore to each other?" Emily's words were soft and tickled in the back of my mind. "We even joked about knocking you out so you could wake up already there." She took a shaky breath. "Take the pill. By the time you wake up, you'll be halfway to Greece. All you have to do is walk with me on board to our seats. The medicine will knock you out before we ever take off."

"If I don't go, you'll never forgive me, will you?" I unhooked my seatbelt, ignoring the strange headache pulsing through my skull. What about that guy at the party that suddenly was in the middle of the road? Was he my guardian angel warning me not to go?

No, it had to be my paranoia playing tricks on me. People

flew all the time. I dug out the sleeping pill and took it with a gulp of my soda. God, I hoped this medicine worked fast.

"We'll always be friends no matter what." She gave me a hug. "But if you don't get on the plane with me, you'll regret it the rest of your life."

"Fine, but if our plane goes down, I'm going to kill you."

CPSIA information can be obtained
at www.ICGtesting.com
Printed in the USA
BVHW031656051119
562978BV00001B/7/P